Slow Transit

Stories by

Michael C. Keith

Červená Barva Press
Somerville, Massachusetts

Červená Barva Press
P.O. Box 440357
W. Somerville, MA 02144-3222

www.cervenabarvapress.com

Bookstore: www.thelostbookshelf.com

Cover image: "Stuifsneeuw.jpg" (Blowing Snow) courtesy Wikimedia Commons

Cover design: William J. Kelle

ISBN: 9780998425368

Library of Congress Control Number: 2017934377

Distributed by Small Press Distribution: www.spdbooks.org

Other Works of Fiction by Michael C. Keith

Perspective Drifts Like a Log on a River

Bits, Specks, Crumbs, Flecks

The Near Enough

If Things Were Made to Last Forever

Caricatures

The Collector of Tears

Everything is Epic

Sad Boy

Of Night and Light

Hoag's Object

And Through the Trembling Air

Life is Falling Sideways

Michael C. Keith is also the author of an acclaimed memoir (*The Next Better Place*) and two-dozen non-fiction titles devoted to the subject of mass communication.

ACKNOWLEDGMENTS

Some of the stories in this collection first appeared in the *Boston Literary Magazine, Literally Stories, Fiction on the Web, The Literary Yard, McStorytellers, Flash Fiction Magazine, Literary Brushstrokes, The Penman Review, Yellow Chair Review, Short-Humour, Intrinsick, Calamities Press, Somerville Times, Fewer than 500, The Commonline Journal, Literary Nest, Funny In Five Hundred, Zero Fiction, Lowestoft Chronicle, Thread,* and *Bougainvillea Literary.*

The author wishes to acknowledge the contributions of Christopher Sterling, Susanne Riette, and Nicki Sahlin.

This collection is dedicated to my wife, Susanne Riette-Keith . . . my forever reader and partner.

TABLE OF CONTENTS

The Start To Mabel's Day   3
Tree   5
An Act of Charity   9
God is Just   16
Senior Faculty Act on Roselle Bixby's Tenure   17
The Story Doubter   20
The Melancholia of Lesser Souls   21
When Nature Changes, Make Lemonade   25
Going the Distance   26
The Major Benefit of Passing   28
When Conversations Take a Turn   29
Sarge   31
Not Prescribed   36
Monk on Fire   40
Dad Leaves   41
2047   46
It's the Gift That Counts   47
Message From the Underground   50
What Happened to Poor Mildred's New Car   52
After   58
Fast Fool   59
Slow Transit   63
The Bequest   64
Two Old Cops Arguing   68
Riding the Serpent   70
Marital Abyss   77
Like a . . .   78
Burying Yourself   80
Nothing Bothers Me   82
Parking Violations   83
Not Ready For Prime Time   86
Personal Development   87
Three Times Under   93
Second Sentences   94

That Deep Sweet Post-Coital Sleep 97
The Decision 98
Solitary Senior 100
Friends in Crime 102
Existential 107
Signings 108
Reader 117
Tot Finder 118
Oops 123
Directions to America 124
Clean Underpants 126
Mascot 127
It Was a Book That Revised Itself 134
The Duke Beat Up the Bad Guys 135
Half Lives 139
Is a Funeral Home *Really* a Home? 141
Indescribable 149
Empty Breathing 150
When You Decide You've Had Enough 152
A Second Opinion 153
Tastes Like 155
Divine Directives 157
An Issue of Image 159
The Substance of Nothing 166
Cold girl 167
My Dear Old Dad 171
Brett's Voice 172
After Admitting That He'd Slept With Her Sister 177
The Pictures on Dorian's Computer 178
The Intransitive 182
Hair Today 183
Rising to the Occasion 185
I'm Still Substance . . . 189
That House 190
Something in Reserve 199
Intimate Apparel Thieves From Outer Space 200
Just an Old Cowhand 201

Why Earthlings Confuse Extraterrestrials   203
The Smell of Distress   204
Exceptional Service   205
Compromise   206
The Too Late Show   208
The 300th   212
Can You Answer This?   217
Number's Up   218
The Trickle Down Effect   223
Acceptance   224
Pro-dactive   226

Author bio

Slow Transit

I travel not to go anywhere. I travel for travel's sake. The great affair is to move.

— Robert Louis Stevenson

Travel far enough, you meet yourself.

— David Mitchell

The Start To Mabel's Day

And then we ease her out of the worn-out body with a
kiss, and she's gone like a whisper, the easiest breath.
                                                    —Mark Doty

The two-room, third floor flat is ice cold. Its radiators no
longer make their loud clanking noise signaling that heat is on
the way. Seventy-eight year old Mabel has wrapped herself in
several layers of clothes in order to keep from freezing, but
she still feels cold. There are mornings she actually considers
remaining in bed rather than deal with the desolation of
another day. The only thing that gets her up is her full
bladder. Once she's relieved herself, she checks the street
below. Visibility is poor because of the ice that has formed on
the inside of the windowpanes. She feels a dull tug in her
abdomen and shuffles to the kitchen. The refrigerator
contains a week old chicken carcass and an empty milk
carton. *I can't put off going to the store any longer*, she tells herself.
She's told herself that for the last three days, and now she
readies herself for the two-block walk by putting on her
shoes. She already has her coat on since she sleeps in it. The
hallway is actually warmer than her flat, and it's as quiet as a
tomb. There's usually some kind of sound coming from
beyond the closed doors—a baby's cry, an adult's shout—but
not this morning. Mabel recalls that it's Sunday. *The store won't*
be open yet, she thinks, and returns to her apartment. On her
way to the chair next to the stove, she feels a sharp pain in
her right knee. It's been getting more difficult to put weight
on it since she slipped on the black ice on the steps leading
into her building a week ago. Before she sits, she strikes a
wooden matchstick and moves it over the stove's gas burners
to take some of the chill away. She warms a kettle for a cup
of instant coffee and peers out of a window again, scraping
the frost away with her thumbnail. A tiny figure in a red coat
is jumping rope on an otherwise empty sidewalk. *Little Margie*
all by yourself again. Your mom has company, I bet. Told you to go

outside and play while she entertains. Well, Mabel's going to come down to keep you company, darling. She's excited by the prospect of meeting up with the neglected child . . . her only friend. At the top of the stairs, she realizes she's left the stove on and quickly changes direction to return to her flat. Her foot catches on the cracked linoleum, causing her to fall backwards down the long flight of stairs. When Mabel hits the bottom landing, she feels warmer than she has since the start of winter. And she remembers a summer's day as a child and her mother's voice calling her name.

#

Tree

Nature conceals what only few see.
                                   —Anonymous

Three months after the sudden death of his 11 year-old son, Ben Devers' mourning took on a whole new and unexpected dimension.

The large oak tree in our backyard attacked and crushed my boy. It was a deliberate act . . . I have no doubt about that, even if my wife says I'm being ridiculous.

"Trees don't think!" growled Karen Devers "They just *are*. Do you think storms deliberately kill people? Jesus, it's *nature*. There's no premeditation or free will involved, Ben. It's bad enough as it is. Stop talking nonsense.

"Calm down, babe. I'm just saying . . ."

"Look, I don't mean to get angry, but your behavior is beginning to unglue me. You believe you can scream at that tree without our neighbors noticing and thinking you've lost it. Please, don't do that anymore. If you're going to act crazy, do it inside the house. In fact, *no* . . . don't do it at all. This has gone as far as it should. Just stop right *now!* Do you hear me? I'm dealing with the loss of our child, too, for God's sake!"

"Yeah, I hear you. Don't blow a gasket. I'll take care of things . . ."

"What do you mean by that?"

"I'm going to cut its limbs off. Disarm it so it doesn't kill me or you . . . or anybody that comes into the yard."

"Okay, that's it! I've got to get away from you. Going to my sisters' for a couple days. You better be over this nonsense when I get back . . . or I'll have to think about leaving for good."

Ben didn't try to dissuade his wife from leaving. In fact, he thought her absence would give him the time he needed to make things right . . . time to avenge his son's death. It was the right thing to do. Indeed, he felt it was the only thing to do.

You can't arrest a tree for homicide and expect it to get what it deserves. It's immune to the laws of society, but I can see that justice is served. I don't care how much it protests. I know it did what it did on purpose. It hated Peter. How many times was he pushed from that scrubby piece of bad timber? No, he didn't just fall from its creaky branches by accident. He was thrown from it. A kid doesn't tumble from a tree as many times as Peter did. It hated him climbing it. Just couldn't deal with it . . . that's obvious.

* * *

After his wife left, Ben walked into the backyard and then around the old oak's trunk as if measuring its circumference.

Wish I could just chop you down, but you're too damn high and wide and would smash whatever you dropped on. Bet you'd like that, wouldn't you—killer that you are?

"I'm not a *killer*," came a voice from the oak tree. "I couldn't help it if one of my branches fell on your boy. Trees have problems with their joints, too. They get rotten just like the sockets in human bodies."

"Sure, you'll speak when my wife isn't around to hear you. Very clever . . . *shrewd.* And don't give me any of that shit

6

about you having arthritis in your limbs. My parents have arthritis in theirs, but their infected body parts don't just drop off. C'mon, don't give me that line of crap. You're a killer, and that's the fact of the matter."

"Look, I've been dealing with rottage. I'm loaded with pathogens and fungi that attack my seams and intersections. I think it's called *Ionontus*, or something like that."

"What a bunch of bull. You tried to murder Peter several times. He kept falling off of you, and not by accident. Not so many times."

"He wasn't a good climber. Clumsy. Couldn't hold on like most kids."

"Now you're saying my son wasn't *normal*? That does it. I'm going to get my saw."

"No . . . no, I'm not saying anything. Maybe I was wet when he was climbing me . . . hard to get a grip then."

"Enough of your lame excuses. Time to give you what you deserve . . . bastard!"

Ben stormed to the shed and returned moments later with his chainsaw.

"Wait . . . wait!" pleaded the oak. "A tree can't do what you're saying. We don't have thoughts, and if we did, I doubt they'd be evil ones. We're not like humans. You kill . . . we don't. Listen to your wife. What did she say before going to her sister's? I think it was, 'Trees don't think. They just *are*'."

"Oh, *you* think, alright. Just listen to you. I wish she could have been around to hear you. You don't fool me. You hated Peter and got rid of him. You're malicious and made it look

7

like an accident. You're a disgrace to your species, or do all you oaks have a streak of the murderer in you?"

"That's *so* wrong, Ben. We don't have consciousness. We just grow and then die, like all things, and we aren't even aware of that."

"You're plenty aware of what you're doing, but you won't be dropping your limbs on any more innocent victims . . . not when I'm through with you."

"I wouldn't do that, Ben. It will get you in trouble with . . ."

"My wife? No way. She knows deep down that you killed our son. If not now, she'll come to realize that soon enough. I'll get her to see the truth."

Ben tugged at the power saw's starter cord a few times before it started roaring. The sound blocked out the oak tree's continuing admonitions.

* * *

Two days later, Karen Devers returned from her sister's place. She searched throughout the house for her husband, and finally found his lifeless body in the backyard. A knobby tree branch rested on him. His severed arm lay on the ground close by, still clutching the power saw.

"Oh, Ben!" wailed Karen. "You *foolish, foolish* man!"

#

An Act of Charity

Wickedness is in the punishment.
    —Francis Quarles

A while back, my wife, Carrie, and I went on a road trip out west to Yellowstone Park. It was the first time we'd ever traveled so far in a car for a vacation. Over four thousand miles round trip from where we live in Maine. We'd talked about it for a long time and finally loaded the car and headed out. We got a Triple A Trip Ticket that had our route highlighted so we wouldn't get off track. We figured 12 days was enough, and that worked out because we both had our two-week summer vacations to use.

Carrie's sister, Millie, was going to feed the cat and collect the papers and mail, so there wasn't anything to fret about when we were away. She'd water the couple of plants we had, too. It was really convenient having her live just up the street whenever we went off somewhere, which actually wasn't too often. I like Millie a lot, and her husband Burt is a good guy——one of my best buddies. They came as an extra benefit to marrying Carrie. That's how I look at it. Burt and me like to go hunting, so during the season, we're out there a lot. That gives the girls plenty of time to do whatever they like.

Anyway, getting back to what I'm writing about here. We were into our third day on the road somewhere in western Nebraska. It was so brown, flat, and empty out there that we hadn't imagined such a place ever existed, except maybe on the moon. Carrie kept asking where the trees were and saying the only time she ever saw so far was when she was looking straight up to the heavens. She was right about that. You could actually see the curve of the earth, because there wasn't anything to block the horizon no matter which way you looked.

It all kind of appealed to me though. The wide-open spaces, that is. Filled me with some kind of awe, you could say. But Carrie wasn't of a like mind on that score. She thought it was way too desolate. Put her off some.

"Where would your friends or family be out here? People can't live in such a place," she said, but then I argued her words by pointing out a house sitting way off from the highway.

"Somebody does," I remarked, and Millie just shrugged her shoulders, saying, "Not me . . . *never*."

Anyway, here's where the story gets interesting and the part that stands out in our minds the most. We pulled into to this rest area to stretch our legs and relieve ourselves, and we see this old car off to the side with its doors wide open. Three kids were running around like they're playing tag and what we figured to be their parents were standing there just looking kind of lost. We parked across from them, and the woman gave us a friendly wave.

We were about to head into the facilities when the man with her called out asking if he could have a word with us. We turned and walked over to where they were parked. When we did, the kids stopped their chasing about and stared at us as if we'd just magically appeared out of thin air.

"Thank you, sir," said the man, extending his hand to shake.

He couldn't have been more than 25, and the woman with him looked even younger. Both had this haggard and wary expression on their faces that gave me the impression that life had not been too easy for them.

"My name's Josh and this is my wife, Carmen. We're in kind of a bind. We ran out of cash on our way home to Laramie and only have enough gas for a few more miles. We thought we were fine, but underestimated what we'd need to get back home. Kids haven't eaten since yesterday, too."

Here the young man took a deep breath that looked to pain him and slowly continued.

"Would it be possible to get a small loan from you? Enough to get us on our way and get the kids a little something to munch on? We'll pay you back as soon as we get home. Just give us your address. You can trust us. This has never happened to us before. Had to get to Kansas City for my mom's funeral, so took off from Laramie half prepared."

My wife gave me a quizzical look, but I could tell that she was feeling sorry for the couple and their brood. They looked like decent enough people to me, so I asked how much they needed. When I looked around, I saw that their kids had resumed their playing near our car.

"Thank you, sir. I figure $20 gas will get us home. If you have another $10 for the kids to get something to put in their bellies, that would be great."

I gave my wife a glance and could tell she was okay with giving them the money. As soon as I reached for my wallet, the woman grabbed my wife's hand and thanked her profusely.

"Please give us your address, so we can mail it right back to you, ma'am," she said.

"No . . . that's okay. Don't worry about it. Glad to help," I said.

"Oh, please let us pay you back," insisted the woman.

"We'll get paid back some other way, dear. A good deed always has its rewards," said Carrie.

"That is tremendously Christian of you," said the man, tucking the bills into his pocket.

"Well, good luck to you and your family," I said, taking Carrie by the hand and moving us in the direction of the restroom facility.

When we returned to our car, there was no sight of the family we'd run into in the parking area. My wife and I sat for a while thinking about the poor folks we'd helped and feeling pretty good about our act of charity.

"It was the right thing to do, honey," said Carrie, squeezing my arm affectionately.

"Yes," I said. "It was the *only* decent thing to do."

That night we had reached Guernsey, Wyoming, where we planned to stay on the last major leg of our west bound road trip. When we gathered our things to take into the motel room we discovered that Carrie's camera was missing.

"Did we leave it back where we stayed in Lincoln?" asked my wife.

"No. I think we contributed more than $30 to those folks back at the rest stop," I answered, thinking of the kids playing around our car while we talked with their parents.

"No . . . really? You think those kids stole it. Well, I can't . . ."

"Hate to think that . . . but, yes, I'm convinced they did. I know your camera was in the back seat."

"Oh, that's just so awful, Terry. Can't imagine anyone putting their children up to stealing from people. What'll we do?"

"Nothing we can do. We don't have their address. All we know is that they were going to Laramie . . . if, in fact, they were."

"We should call the police."

"And what would we tell them? We don't even know their names."

On our return home after having had a great time in Yellowstone, we stopped at the same roadside rest area where we'd had our bad experience. Just for the heck of it I asked the attendant if she remembered seeing the couple we'd run into. She gave us a surprised expression and then lifted a bag from behind the counter.

"You the people who left this behind?" asked the woman, removing Carrie's camera from a sack.

To say the least, we were more than a little stunned. "Yes, it's ours. But how . . .?"

"A young couple said they found it in the parking lot and hoped you might come back and get it. And, Lord almighty, here you are. Isn't that just the darnedest thing?"

"Did they say anything else?"

"Not at that time, but they came back a few days later and told me to put this envelope in the bag with the camera."

Still in shock, we thanked the attendant and returned to our car. There I opened the envelope and found a piece of paper with handwriting on it and three 10 dollar bills.

The note read as follows:

Our oldest child has a problem with taking things that don't belong to him. When we got back home, we found your camera, and he confessed to stealing it from your car. We feel so bad and hope you come back to that rest stop so you can get your valuable. We're still not sure what to do with our child's problem, but we hope returning your camera shows him how to right a very bad wrong. We may have to tie him up in the basement until the devil is out of him. Bless you and thank you for your kindness. God be with you always.

"Oh Lord, they wouldn't do that to their child, would they, Terry? That would be so cruel."

"No . . . I doubt it. They're probably just joking about tying him up."

"Well, they didn't strike me as the joking type. We have to try to get in touch with them."

"There's no way we can find them, honey. There's no address on this envelope."

"Maybe they left it with the attendant. Let's go ask."

We checked back with the lady in the rest stop, but she said the young couple hardly spoke a word when they dropped off the camera and later the envelope. Carrie was so upset at the possibility that a child might be abused on her account that she even suggested we go toward Laramie and try to track down the family. But I convinced her that it would be like looking for a needle in a haystack without having their names, and we continued on home to Maine.

This all happened nearly three years ago now, and we've pretty much put the whole thing out of our minds. But every so often it comes up in conversation—and we start worrying about that kid all over again.

#

God is Just

A small space rock struck the Seibold's trailer and landed on Mary Lou's abusive husband. It was at that exact moment she accepted the Lord as her savior.

#

Senior Faculty Act on Roselle Bixby's Tenure

In [Academia] the only homage they pay to virtue is hypocrisy.
—Lord Byron

Full Professor Seymour Wilkes had planned to vote against the tenure of assistant professor Bixby in any case. While he admitted to himself that she was amply qualified for the distinction based on her excellent record of publications and teaching evaluations, he simply didn't like her—mainly he disapproved of her appearance. To him, her short skirts and modestly tattooed forearm were the deal breakers. *She just doesn't look respectable. Looks too much like some of our students, and she acts like she prefers their company to ours.*

Department Chair Daniel Mayer also pushed for a negative outcome for Bixby. He believed there were already too many women in the department, which he felt had resulted a preponderance of courses with a feminist bias. *Sure she deserves a favorable vote, but I'll be damned if I'll let women determine the direction of this program. She's just proposed a new course with an obvious gender studies bent*—Male Domination in Architectural Design: The Ascending Phallus and the Lowering of the Glass Ceiling. *What utter bullshit!*

As was the case with her senior counterparts, Full Professor Constance Oberlin had her own reasons for voting nay on the tenure decision. Her view overlapped with Wilkes'. Like him, she felt the aspirant's casual, if not provocative, wardrobe and carefree bearing were inappropriate for a member of the professoriate. At bottom, however, Oberlin was envious of the tenure candidate's attractiveness and popularity with her students. *She's a little too familiar with the boys. They love her, but I don't understand why the girls do, too. Anyway, she's a distraction that we just don't need here. Let her take her pretty face somewhere else.*

Associate Professor Cynthia Carson had her own self-serving rationale for blocking Bixby's tenure. The fact that the candidate had top tier journal articles and a book about to be published by a major university press fueled Carson's own formidable insecurities. She'd gotten tenure two decades earlier with only a few minor publications, which would surely keep her from gaining tenure in the current academic environment. Carson had done little since being tenured, and that failure kept her from promotion to full professor. *Bixby will end up outranking me, and she'll even become chair, too. We've never been very friendly, so I'll probably get the lousy committees and crummy teaching schedules. And who knows how she'll treat me in my annual faculty evaluations. No, she can't remain here.*

At first, Full Professor Jennifer Hanson was somewhat conflicted as to how she should vote on Bixby. Part of her knew the young faculty member deserved tenure and the "job for life" that came with it, because she had actually exceeded the university's stated tenure expectations. However, the less magnanimous part of her personality felt that Bixby cozied up to the administration, especially the institutions' influential vice president. *He acts really taken by her, and it's obvious that she flirts with him—a clever little one . . . that one. Knows what buttons to push to get what she wants. I don't think I'm imagining that she has big ambitions. So in good conscience, I can't vote for her.*

In the end, the department was unanimous in recommending denial of tenure for Roselle Bixby. When the university's final decision came down a few months later, Bixby was upset but ultimately relieved by it. Appeal was the last thing on her mind.

I can't imagine working with these assholes for the rest of my career anyway.

By the following academic year, Bixby had joined the faculty of the more prestigious Duke University. When she bumped into her old colleagues at a conference a few months into the semester, she told them in no uncertain terms what she thought of them.

"Well, we obviously made the right decision about her!" blustered Full Professor Wilkes.

"Yes, she clearly would have been trouble with a capital T . . . and that stands for *tenure*," snickered Chairman Mayer.

"Did you see what she was wearing? Apparently, they don't care how she struts around at Duke," observed Full Professor Oberlin.

"She would have caused me, ur . . . *us* problems if we'd voted her tenure," offered Associate Professor Carson.

"In my opinion, Bixby had an agenda that went far beyond the department," added Full Professor Hanson.

After a brief pause, the senior faculty congratulated themselves on the wisdom of their decision.

#

The Story Doubter

Is it a good story? questioned the young writer.

No, it's a bad story, thought the young writer.

Why do I bother to write? questioned the young writer.

Maybe it's not so bad, thought the young writer.

Will it get published? questioned the young writer.

It's just not good enough, thought the young writer.

Why do I even try? questioned the young writer.

The plot could be stronger, thought the young writer.

Should I submit it now? questioned the young writer.

The characters are not credible, thought the young writer.

Where would I send it? questioned the young writer.

It'll just get rejected, thought the young writer.

Should I revise it? questioned the young writer.

I'll give it another read, thought the young writer.

Wow, why did I doubt my writing? questioned the young writer.

The New Yorker *will probably take it,* thought the young writer.

#

The Melancholia of a Lesser Soul

*You can't be admitted to the ranks of writers
of importance unless you have sales.*
                              —James Salter

It didn't appear to matter to the world at large that he'd published two books of poetry and another of short stories. At least that's what Gil Porter had come to believe. He'd been certain that when his first book of verse appeared on Amazon, considerable attention, if not fame, would follow— a naïve notion, he quickly came to realize. Several weeks had passed with only a handful of people, mostly friends, offering comments (superlative in nature, of course) on the cyber bookstore site. There were no official reviews on the web or in any print publications—as far as he knew. *Damn, hoped I'd have sold a few more copies than that! Sure, poetry has a limited audience, but jeez* . . . thought Gil, staring grimly at his computer monitor.

Gil had joined a local writers group by the time he'd gathered enough poems for a second collection. Being able to commiserate with fellow scribes about the problems of getting the general public to buy poetry chapbooks buoyed him but did not dispel his disappointment. Nonetheless, he moved ahead and found a small press to put out his second volume. While he didn't have to put up any advance money to get it published, the tiny press expected him to purchase a number of copies (at an author's discount) to help cover its expenses. *At least it's not self-published,* he told himself, but wondered if that were entirely true. *Would they publish my book if I didn't agree to offset some of their costs?*

When his second volume of poems appeared, he gave readings in a couple of venues that were mostly attended by members of his own writing group. *Like preaching to the choir,* he thought, but he did enjoy the experience and received warm praise from those who were present. But once again few people outside of his immediate sphere of writers took notice of his new publication. In fact, to his considerable chagrin, even fewer readers left reviews on Amazon than for his first collection. Likewise, as before, not a single critique of his work appeared in other publications.

Gil began to question the quality of his verse and considered pursuing other avenues of creative expression. He also came to the conclusion that there was just too much poetry available to the reading audience, which he knew was small to begin with. He'd written a couple of short stories before devoting himself to verse and decided to turn his attention back to that genre. Happily he found that story writing came easily, and he was quick to find a receptive market for his prose in a wide variety of webzines—of which there seemed an endless number.

Much sooner than he anticipated he found he had enough pieces for a collection, and once again he prospected for a small commercial press to publish it. At first he considered sending the manuscript to a large trade house but the realization quickly sunk in that without an agent or an established name the likelihood of finding success was slim to nonexistent. He'd read that the big presses were not eager to publish short story collections, even by their own bestselling authors.

It took a while, but he ultimately located a small publisher in California willing to take on his first prose collection and, surprisingly, it didn't expect him to purchase a ton of copies. In short order the book appeared, but as with his two previous titles, it went nowhere —no reviews, no fanfare. As with his books of verse, the publisher did not have the resources to market its catalog. In the end, Gil calculated that he'd sold about 35 copies of his story collection, a figure not any better than his poetry books.

Gil had always enjoyed spending time in bookstores, but since his own titles never appeared in the brick and mortar outlets, he began to avoid them. It was just too depressing for him to deal with the absence of his works on their shelves. He began to resent the authors whose titles did make it into the stores. *Admit it, you're just a no count scribbler . . . a frigging nobody. Only the big publishers get their writers into Barnes & Noble or independent booksellers. Good luck to the rest of us.*

When he complained about the situation to his writer's group colleagues, he was reminded that online sites and e-readers had replaced traditional bookstores. But to Gil, if his titles weren't physically present in bookstores, they only had half an existence . . . if that.

"Your thinking is old school, Gil. Most people go online to buy books in this day and age. That's just the way it is today, so if your books are on Amazon, they've made it. It's the biggest bookstore in the world, and your books are featured there," declared a member of his writer's group.

"Yeah, but there are millions of titles on Amazon, so how does the public find yours? The bestselling authors come from places with promotion budgets, like Scribner and Knopf, not presses like East Elephant Trunk Books, with only their own website to get word out about their new titles."

"So why do you write if you're so down on the whole thing? Is it just for the money? You can't be writing to get rich. You know that only one or two percent of the writing population makes a living doing it."

"No, that's not it. But I'd like a little more recognition for my work. There's so much crap out there that's selling because it gets publicity. Quality doesn't seem to matter."

"Then you should concentrate on getting a big name publisher."

"You know that they don't want short story or poetry collections. They're like rotting fish to those guys."

"Then why don't you write a novel or do non-fiction?"

"Hey, I love the short fiction form. I'm not interested in writing anything else."

"Well, if you *love* writing short stories, why are you so unhappy? At least what you do is getting into print. Look around, Gil, many of us aren't even getting published. You're doing better than most of us. Damn, I'd give my eyeteeth to get my fiction published . . . even by a small indie press. You should be thankful they exist. I don't need a Doubleday or Simon and Schuster to court me. I'd be perfectly happy to be a so-called *low-list* author."

"That's what you think now, but when you become one, you'll be as gloomy as a Stephen King story . . . without his royalties.

"Look, why don't you just give up writing altogether, Gil? Maybe that would make you feel better about your life."

"Are you kidding? Don't be ridiculous. Writing *is* my life."

#

(The title was inspired by a commentary on the literary achievements of Kurt Vonnegut in *STOPSMILING: The Magazine for High-Minded Lowlifes*, No. 27, "Ode to the Midwest.")

When Nature Changes, Make Lemonade

Throughout the autumn everyone waited for the leaves to change color, but they didn't. The businesses in New England that depended on the revenue from visiting leaf peepers were in a virtual frenzy. This had never happened before. Even in the worst of situations, there had been some show of color. To make matters even more dismaying, in just a single day all of the green leaves fell from their trees. This caused an assortment of problems, not the least among them clogged storm drains and packed roof gutters and downspouts. Before anyone could deal with the perplexing issue, the skies darkened, temperatures plunged, and it snowed . . . in *color*, covering all of the fallen leaves in splashes of radiant orange, red, brown, purple, blue, and magenta. When word got out, leaf peepers swarmed north to catch the transformation before it melted. Suddenly retailers were counting their profits while excited tourists rejoiced in the change of season.

#

Going the Distance

There is something curiously boring about somebody else's happiness.
—Aldous Huxley

Miranda loved the coastline of New England, while her husband, Charlie, preferred the wide-open spaces of western Nebraska. After a relatively short discussion about where they'd spend their retirement years, an agreement was reached: Half of the year would be spent on the New England shoreline. And the other half of the year would also be spent on the New England shoreline.

After three years of quiet repose to the sound of seagulls and surf, Miranda passed away. A week following her funeral, Charlie booked a flight to Omaha and then rented a car. Six hours later he reached Alliance, a small town located on the high plains of the far Midwest.

Shortly after arriving, he bought a modest house a dozen miles out of the center. He felt he had finally fulfilled a long time dream as he sat on the porch watching the sun set on the unobstructed horizon.

In time, Charlie joined the senior center in town, and during a bean supper on a Friday evening, he met Sandra, a fellow septuagenarian. Not long after, he fell in love with her and proposed. To his great satisfaction, she accepted, and they began life in her larger house on the outskirts of the business district.

Life was better than Charlie ever thought it could be, until a revelation by his new wife on their first month anniversary caught him off guard.

"I've always dreamed of living close to the ocean. Maybe right on the beach," confided Sandra. "I'm not sure I'll ever feel fulfilled unless I do."

Realizing that her deep-seated yearning would most likely have a negative impact on their life together, Charlie decided to take action.

"Darling, you know I want us to be happy, so I bought you something I think will guarantee that," said Charlie, handing his wife an envelope.

Sandra opened it excitedly, but when she saw what was inside, she was perplexed.

"It's a single *one-way* ticket to the East Coast."

"Exactly," said Charlie.

#

The Major Benefit of Passing

It will be such a relief when my death is behind me. All my life I've dreaded it, but when it happens, it will be one less thing to worry about.

#

When Conversations Take a Turn

"If I had the choice between staring at a ceiling for eternity or the breathless nothingness of death, which would I choose? Is that what you're asking me?"

"Exactly," answered Beth. "It's a simple enough question, Clay. Would you rather continue to live no matter how barren your existence, or would you prefer total oblivion?"

"Christ, where do you come up with these things? Do you lie awake at night thinking what kind of crazy shit can I ask people?"

"Actually, I don't. Things just pop into my head, but they usually have a source, a point of origin. For instance, last year when I was in the hospital for sepsis and thought the end was near, I was gazing up at the ceiling—you know, one of those suspended jobs . . . a dropped ceiling, I think they call them. It had all these tiny perforations in the white squares that were hanging from metal straps."

"And that's when you thought about the question you just asked me?" inquired Clay, drawing on a joint and passing it over.

"Thanks. Yeah, I thought I'd rather spend forever looking at anything at all and remain alive. At least I would still be around . . . you know, present. Not gone forever."

"You're talking about gawking up at a frigging hospital ceiling for eternity just so you can keep on breathing?"

"Right. You got it. If you had to make up your mind right now whether to do that or become extinct, what would you choose?"

"Jesus, that's a really heavy ask. I might opt for life if it were a popcorn ceiling.

"*Popcorn?* What's that?"

"You know, those ceilings with little lumps that look like cottage cheese. Hey, I'm getting hungry . . . *you?*"

"Huh? Yeah, what do you have?" replied Beth.

#

Sarge

*I think you can honour the sacrifices of a common soldier without
glorifying war.*
—Geraldine Brooks

It's 1962 and I'm into my seventh month as a supply room
clerk at a missile base on the coastline of the Yellow Sea in
Korea when Sergeant Brennan shows up. He's my former
boss's replacement, and he's a lot older than I expect. We
shake hands, and I notice a scar running the length of his left
cheek. His eyes are watery, and he looks exhausted, like he
hasn't slept in days.

"Good to meet you, Specialist Keith," he says, his hand damp
and limp.

"Mike, Sarge," I say.

"Yeah, okay . . . Sarge is fine. Call me *Sarge*, Mike."

He drops his sagging body into the chair behind the desk he
figures is his and then asks what's on tap for the day.

"About to hit the road to make my rounds," I answer.

My primary job is to drive the supply truck up to ASCOM
City (a military distribution center) to pick up base supplies,
mostly laundry and food for the guard dogs. It takes me from
around 0900 until mid-afternoon to make the run, and I do it
five days a week. I'm glad to be out on the road on my own.
Sitting in the supply room makes me antsy, and already I
think it would be worse with this lifer in my face.

"Oh," he says, making it sound more like a question. "You
drive the supply truck."

"Do it every day, Sarge."

"Good, well, I'll familiarize myself with things while you're gone and probably have lots of questions when you get back," he says, and begins to cough loudly.

When I return to the base around 1530 hours, the supply room is empty. I look for Sarge, but the guy who runs the medic's station across the hall tells me that he's gone to his room in the NCO quarters.

"He wasn't feeling too good. Gave him some APCs," says my buddy, Corporal Rick Mosley, when I ask. "Think he's got a drinking problem. Looks like a rummy. Could smell booze on him."

* * *

The next morning I'm getting ready to head out and Sarge shows up looking none too steady.

"Morning," he says, going directly to the pot of coffee I just made and pouring himself a cup.

His hand shakes as he lifts the mug to his lips.

"You okay, Sarge?"

"Sure, still getting my legs back after 20 days on the Breck," he says.

"I came over on the *Breckenridge*, too," I respond enthusiastically, but he doesn't seem to hear me.

"Was supposed to fly here, but things got screwed up. Didn't feel right as soon as that ship left Oakland. Couldn't keep anything down. Same as the last time."

"Were you here during the war?" I ask.

He begins to cough again, and it causes the contents of his cup to spill on his fatigues.

"Goddamn it," he growls, wiping at his shirt and then his mouth.

There's blood on his handkerchief, and he notices that I've noticed, and he tucks it into his pocket.

"Was here when the shit was flying, son. Not such a nice place to be back then. Hell of a lot better now from the look of things. Got a little banged up when I was here the last time," he says, running his finger over his scar.

"Must have been real bad," I say, and gather my things for my day on the road.

"Wasn't good," says Sarge, as I'm on my way out of the supply room. "Got pretty ugly. Stay out of the wars if you can, Mike, or you'll end up like me"

The sound of his hacking follows me half way to the motor pool. *Poor guy*, I think, wondering how his full story must read.

* * *

The following week I'm sitting at my desk and suddenly Sarge collapses. When I reach him, his face is already turning blue and there's foam bubbling from his lips. "Rick," I shout. "Get in here, Sarge is in trouble."

The medic shows up in a matter of seconds and surveys the situation. By now I'm worried that Sarge is dead.

"Christ!" he blurts. "Damned if I'll give him mouth-to-mouth," says Rick. "Be right back."

He returns in a minute with an oxygen tank and places its mask on Sarge's face. To my great relief, he comes around almost immediately. By now, the captain is in the supply room having heard the uproar from his office down the hall.

"Get the ambulance truck, Rick, and get him to the hospital."

I accompany both medic and patient to the medical facility in Seoul. On the way, Sarge is in and out of consciousness, but by the time we reach the hospital, he seems a lot better and asks us to take him back to the base.

"Can't do it. The captain ordered us to bring you here. You need to be checked over," says Rick.

"C'mon, guys. I'm fine. Just got a little dizzy is all. I'm okay, really."

Despite Sarge's claims, the attending doctor thinks otherwise, and he is checked in for tests. We return to our base, and several days pass before we're told he is being shipped back to the states for more extensive treatment. Whatever his medical problem is, we never hear.

"Don't know what the hell is going on with Brennan," says our First Sargent, when I ask for more details. "Guy's a hard drinker. Think the sauce is killing him. Too bad, he's really paid his dues. Took some hard hits during the wars."

"*Wars*, Sarge?" I ask.

"Yup, he served in World War Two *and* Korea. Got a bronze star and two purple hearts. Poor bastard deserves better. Real damn hero. Think it screwed him up good. Lousy personal life. Divorce and all that shit. It's why he stayed active so long. Should have retired long ago, but no place else to go, I guess."

Later, I sit in Rick's office, and we both agree that Sarge got a raw deal in life.

"Man, it's a heck of a way to end up after going through what he did," I say, adding that I hope he'll be okay.

"He seemed like a good guy. Reminded me of my uncle. He used to hit the booze pretty hard, too, after his wife died. Maybe he'll get help back home. Sad how some guys end up," remarks Rick.

* * *

Two weeks later, the base commander catches me as I'm walking to my truck to start my day, and he tells me that Sarge died of a brain hemorrhage on his way back to the states. It was news I couldn't shake from my thoughts as I drove through the bleak winter countryside of South Korea.

Now, more than a half-century later, I can still see Sarge lying there on the supply room floor as if it all happened yesterday. The memory I have of *that* old soldier is still vivid. General MacArthur had it wrong; some old soldiers *never* fade away. I hadn't read much back then, but something that must have come out of a book filled my head as I made my designated stops the day I was told that Sarge had died: "It's so much darker when even a dim light goes out."

#

Not Prescribed

About half of all people don't take medications
like they're supposed to.

—Eric Topol

Marissa Harding took a boatload of pills each day to keep the maladies of old age in check. She had not taken prescription drugs of any sort until she hit 70 when arthritis began to attack her joints and cause her pain. Within the same year she had been prescribed meds for an irregular heartbeat, COPD stemming from a life long cigarette habit, and another med for progressive osteoporosis that was beginning to bend her body. *What a grievous tsunami of ailments,* she lamented.

Just one year later, she was diagnosed with diabetes, resulting in an additional pill. Later that same year, she was given prescriptions for a chronic inner ear disease that caused dizziness, another for tendinitis that resulted in swollen ankles, and two more for acid reflux and cystitis respectively. In all Marissa was downing 21 capsules and tablets a day by her 78th birthday.

This regimen had become a worry and expense to her and one morning she decided to stop taking the pills to hasten her demise. *Why live like this? I feel like an ancient ruin and half the time I can't think clearly because of all the drugs in my system. My quality of life is gone. It's time to go,* thought Marissa, dumping her day's worth of meds into the commode and flushing it. *There, I feel better already.*

By the end of the day, she felt no different than she had that morning. In fact, her appetite seemed better than it had in months. *Probably all those chemicals were making me less hungry. By God, I think I'll order a pizza. May be my last supper. So I go out of this world with a little heartburn . . . so what? At least I'll die happy.*

To put it mildly, Marissa was surprised that she was still among the living the next morning. She had devoured half of a peperoni pizza and two glasses of wine before going to bed and had slept the entire night without getting up several times, as was the usual case. *My lands, I'm still here, and I think I'm okay*, she told herself, climbing from under the covers and putting on her robe and slippers.

Again, she flushed her day's load of pills down the toilet. After washing her face and wiping it with a generous amount of Pond's Cold Cream, she proceeded to the kitchen where, for the first time in several years, she made a pot of coffee. *They said to stay away from caffeine. That it would cause me all kinds of problems, so maybe a couple strong cups will set me free from my world of troubles. Fill it up with plenty of sugar and cream, too, Marissa, old gal.*

Contrary to her expectations, she actually felt more energized as the day grew shorter. *No sign of things starting to go wrong. No symptoms. Isn't that amazing? Now why would that be? My doctor told me that all these pills were keeping me alive. So how come I'm not dead yet? In fact, I'm actually feeling better than I did when I was taking them according to his directions.*

At suppertime, Marissa ordered three different dishes of Chinese takeout and gobbled down most of them. When she noticed that it was 8 PM, her normal bedtime, she was pleased that she felt no fatigue whatsoever. *Now isn't that something? Heck, I'll watch some of those later TV shows. Haven't seen Johnny Carson in years.*

It was after midnight when Marissa finally turned in, and she slept soundly until nearly 9 the next morning. *My, oh my, I'm starving. Would love a cheese omelet*, she thought, rising quickly from bed. Once again she disposed of her daily dose of pills and marveled at how well she felt since she stopped taking them. *Should have done this a long time ago.*

Marissa began to think that her doctor had been wrong to put her on so many meds and that maybe he had done so to keep her dependent on him. *He's probably in cahoots with those big pharmaceutical companies. Maybe all the old people doctors are in it together to get rich off of us,* considered Marissa, as she cracked open several eggs and poured their contents into a bowl.

Several days passed with Marissa continuing to forsake her medicines. Despite this, she felt fine and experienced no negative reactions. *All those specialists I've been sent to just wanted me hooked on their prescriptions so I'd keep spending money and stay alive long enough for them to pay for their vacation homes in the Bahamas.*

On the day that marked the one-week anniversary of Marissa's abstinence from her multitude of meds, she climbed into her dusty and unused car and drove to Monster Burger for lunch. It had been 4 years since she'd eaten out, and the prospect of doing so excited her. On her way, she managed to sideswipe several parked vehicles and run three red lights without even knowing it.

I'm a new person since I stopped taking those stupid pills. After I have lunch, I'm going to drive over to my primary care doctor's office and give him a piece of my mind. Maybe I should report his scheme to the newspaper. How dare he treat old folks like this? We have a right to live without the bad affects of all those chemicals they put us on. It's a horrible thing to be doing to people who've reached their so-called golden years.

When Marissa arrived at Monster Burger she ordered its Super Colossal Cheeseburger with fries and a large vanilla milkshake and found a table in which to consume it in peace. *Lordy, this smells so good. Jeez, imagine that. I can even smell things better since I've been off all those dratted pills.*

The manager of the fast food restaurant had not noticed the elderly woman at the far table until closing time. When he approached her, he immediately felt something was wrong. *Oh my God! I think she's dead*, he thought.

"Ma'am . . . *ma'am?*" he ventured and was startled when he got a response.

"Oh, I'm sorry. I must have dozed off. Can I get another Super Colossal Cheeseburger and vanilla shake?"

#

Monk on Fire

Douse me . . . please.

Douse me now.

Strike the match.

Let me light the world.

(Thich Quang Duc burned himself to death at a busy intersection in Saigon in 1963. He was protesting the U.S. supported regime of Ngo Dinh Diem, which had long been persecuting the country's Mahayana Buddhist monks.)

#

Dad Leaves

I think childhood is, generally speaking, a preparation
for disappointment.
                                        —Seamus Heaney

My Dad was making his last visit before he left for Rochester. He claimed he had a great job lined up there, but Mom didn't believe him. She gave him permission to see my brother and me before he set out for a place that sounded far off and exotic to us. Almost 6 months had passed since she'd thrown him out of our apartment for drinking, and we'd only seen him twice since then.

We'd spotted Dad down on Baskins Street coming out of a bar. He was half in the bag but caught sight of us before we could hide. Neither Chris nor I wanted to be around him when he was on the bottle. The other time we saw him was on Easter. He came by with a big basket of hard boiled eggs that he said he'd won playing darts over at Muldoon's Saloon. Mom said it was the only time he came out of that gin joint with something besides empty pockets. But later she threw them out saying that only God knew how old they were.

When Dad showed up to say goodbye, he was sober, and we were really happy about that. We knew Mom would blow her top if he even smelled of booze. He had on a clean white shirt and smelled of Old Spice After Shave. That scent is something I always liked and still do today, although I don't wear it myself—too old world . . . and cheap. At least that's how I think of it. My wife says that when drugstores stock men's cologne they do so as a quick fix for customers who've been up to no good. Indeed, she and Mom saw eye-to-eye on most things.

"Hey, there, Billy and Chris. Whoa, I think you guys grew a foot since I saw you," said my Dad, ruffling our hair as we stood in the doorway.

At first, we both felt a little awkward around him, but we were still glad to see him.

"So, you going to invite me in? Your Mom wants me to visit you here instead of going out some place. Where is she, by the way?"

Mom said she didn't want to see him, so she stayed in her room during the visit. We escorted Dad into the front room and sat on the couch across from him.

"She can really be hard-headed . . . that woman. Well, who needs to see her anyway, right?" said Dad, with a half-smile.

We didn't respond, and, to our relief, Dad changed the subject. We didn't like him saying stuff about Mom, any more than when she said stuff about him. But they nearly always ended up saying something mean about each other.

"Well, your old Dad has got a great new job and is leaving this afternoon on the Greyhound. Not crazy about living in upstate New York, but it's a good opportunity."

"How long does it take to get to Chester, Dad?" asked my little brother.

"*Rochester*, Chris. Oh, I'd say about six hours, depending on how many stops the bus makes."

"Will you come back to visit us?" I asked.

"Heck, yes. I wouldn't abandon my boys. Did your Mom say I wasn't coming back? Don't listen to her. You're my sons, and I'm not going to just disappear on you."

"Can we come see you in Ches . . . I mean, Rochester, Dad?"

"Sure, maybe when I get situated. Haven't got a permanent place there yet. But as soon as I do, I'll talk to your Mom about coming out. It'll be up to her though. She's not too keen on me being alone with you boys. I don't know what she thinks will happen. I'm not going to drink anymore, if that's what she's all riled up about."

"Mom doesn't like you to drink, Dad," said Chris.

"We don't either," I added.

"Well, I'm not. And you can tell her that, since she won't see me so I can tell her myself."

For the next half hour, we exchanged small talk, mostly about what we'd been up to and his new job selling tires at his friend's store.

"You remember, Bernie? He was here last year. He gave you boys money when the ice cream truck came around."

I did recall that, but mostly what I remembered was my Dad and his friend getting pretty loaded and my mother being really pissed about it. A few months later, my Dad moved out while we were sleeping.

"He's opening a second store, and your old man may manage it . . . if all goes according to plan."

My brother and me nodded our approval, and while I figured Chris was genuinely impressed by the prospect of our father being a big deal boss, I couldn't help but think that this would *not* go according to plan. Nothing really ever went according to plan with him.

"Well, I guess I better get going so I don't miss my bus."

"Where's your suitcase, Dad?" I asked.

"Left it in a locker at the depot instead of carrying it around," he answered, rising from his chair.

I wondered if he even had a suitcase, because he had a leather shaving kit with him, which I figured would have been stored in the locker, too. Despite my doubt, I said nothing, and walked him to the door.

"Now you guys be good for your Mom. Don't get in any trouble. Won't be able to visit you in jail, if you do."

It was at that point my little brother began to cry.

"Hey, fella, no blubbering, okay? I'm not going forever. Billy, you tell your Mom I'll be back to visit real soon. And tell her to let you guys come and visit me in Rochester. Would you like that, Chris?"

"Yes," he gulped, wiping the tears from his cheek.

"You take care of your little brother, Billy. You're the man of the house while I'm gone."

The sound of the word *gone* made me choke up a little, too, but I didn't let on that I was also upset that he was leaving for a place I was certain I'd never see.

"I will," I said, putting my arm around my brother to console him as much as to console myself.

"Okay, then. I'll see you soon . . . all right, you two?" he said, patting both of our cheeks.

"Bye, Dad," mumbled Chris, backing away.

"Tell your old lady I'll be in touch with her soon."

With that he left. Just two months later he was back saying the job in Rochester didn't work . . . according to plan.

#

2047

Harold Carpenter sat nervously in the waiting room for his appointment with the oncologist. He had been administered a series of tests for his inexplicable weight loss and the dark area spotted in his chest. *It's probably pancreatic cancer,* he thought, growing impatient for his meeting with the doctor. *Jesus, I hope not . . . anything but that. It's such a miserable thing to go through.*

"Mr. Carpenter, the doctor will see you now," said the receptionist.

Oh, God, here we go. Brace yourself, ol' buddy. Gird your loins. This could be the worst news ever, he brooded, as he entered the tumor specialist's office.

"Mr. Carpenter, please have a seat. We do have the results of your tests and we're ready to deal with it."

"So, it's what I thought . . . pancreatic cancer?" said Harold, exhaling deeply.

"I'm afraid so."

"So that means . . .?"

"Yes, you'll have to take two of these pills a day for the next week and you'll be cured."

"But I hear they leave such a bitter taste in your mouth, Doc!" whined Harold.

#

It's the Gift That Counts

The best gift of all is money, because you don't have to wrap it.
—Curtis Blais

Every time a Christmas commercial for Mercedes, Cadillac, or BMW came on television, it boggled Barry Sudbury's mind to think that there actually were people in the viewing audience who could cough up $100K for a present. *Jesus,* he thought, *those damn cars cost more than my house.* It filled him with envy and resentment that he could barely afford something from Wal-Mart to give his wife when there were individuals who had the wherewithal to spend more money on holiday gifts than all of his assets combined, including his retirement fund.

"So you want a Caddy for Christmas, honey?" Barry asked his wife, who stopped her knitting to answer.

"No, actually I'd prefer a Jaguar" she replied, after a thoughtful pause. "More sporty."

They both chuckled, and Amy Sudbury returned to the scarf she was making.

"Really, how can anyone afford to give a luxury car as a Christmas present, for chrissakes?"

"Well, those folks in the TV commercial can."

"They're actors, Amy."

"So, actors make a lot of money."

"But they're not *real* people. You think if they had enough dough to buy expensive cars as gifts they'd be acting in stupid commercials?"

"Maybe you're right, Barry."

"Of course, I'm right."

At that moment, the Sudbury's doorbell rang, and Amy went to answer it.

"It's Billy, sweetheart," she called, finding her son standing before her.

"What's he doing here? I thought he was arriving tomorrow," said Barry, rising from his recliner with a grunt.

"Hello, Mother," said Billy, wrapping his arms around her. "I came early to be here when the present I bought for you and Dad arrived. They should be here any minute."

"Hey, Billy, you're looking prosperous," observed Barry, running his hand down the sleeve of his son's black cashmere coat.

"Yeah, it's been a *really* good year for me."

As the Sudbury's were standing in the entranceway, a bright red Cadillac pulled up.

"Oh, good, it's here," said Billy enthusiastically. "Come on."

Barry suddenly stiffened as if jabbed with a cattle prod. "You mean you got us . . .? No way. Holy crap! Like those people in the commercials? Really . . . *really?*"

"Huh, Dad? What are you . . .? Let's get your present. I had it delivered."

"This is too much, son. You shouldn't have . . ."

Billy led his parents to the waiting car and opened its door.

"Thanks for delivering these, Hal. I couldn't get to the store in time. You're a true bud. I owe you."

"Wha . . .?" moaned Barry."

"What's the matter, Dad? I thought you loved Hickory Farm gift baskets."

#

Message From the Underground

Where you used to be, there is a hole in the world, which I find myself constantly walking around in the daytime, and falling in at night.

—Edna St. Vincent Millay

Kay Holland slipped a freshly charged cellphone into her deceased father's coffin. The thought of never being able to communicate with him again caused her pain beyond anything she'd ever experienced. There had hardly been a day in her 37 years that she and her father hadn't been in contact——a morning call to say hello and wish her a great day had in recent years become a cellphone text loaded with affectionate emojis that never failed to raise her spirits.

In the four days since her father's sudden death, the absence of his daily message deepened Kay's profound sense of loneliness and loss. The anguish was almost unbearable, and without close relations with others to help ease it, she began to feel life wasn't worth living. Her father had been the bedrock of her existence since the passing of her mother and sister in a car accident and the breakup of her marriage.

She told no one about secreting an iPhone under her father's head in the hope they might resume communication. Even she felt it was a strange thing to do, but she couldn't help herself. If there was any chance at all that she might renew contact with him, it was worth doing in her mind. She had taken solace in the stories she'd heard about the dead making contact with the living, so it did not seem beyond the realm of possibility.

Thus every morning following her father's burial, Kay had sent him a text —*luv you, Dad . . . miss U so much . . . thinking of U* . . . And every morning she would wait patiently for a reply—which would not come. However, the simple act of messaging him heartened her and made her feel less forlorn.

Soon she was texting her father several times a day, thinking that the more she did the greater the chance he might respond. And she was right. When her cellphone pinged, she was startled, because she rarely, if ever, got texted. *Could it be? Oh, my God, please let it be him!* she thought.

Her hands trembled as she pressed the message icon. "Dad, it's you . . . it's really you?" she yelped with joy upon seeing the text. And then her glee quickly turned to hurt as she read her father's words:

"Luv and miss U, 2, honey. But for God's sake, Kay, give me a little peace and quiet, would you?"

#

What Happened to Poor Mildred's New Car

Sometimes the heart sees what is invisible to the eye.
                    —H. Jackson Brown, Jr.

My neighbor, Mildred, saved up forever to buy one of them little baby Fiats. You know, the ones that look like pregnant roller skates and come in those puny colors that seem faded already. I have to admit they are kind of cute, but I'd hate to take one on the highway. Damn, I think a passing 18-wheeler would blow you the hell off the road. They don't look like they'd take a hard gust of wind and stay put.

Mildred was so excited with her new set of wheels though. She kept talking about it as if it was the greatest thing ever happened to her. Probably was, because she doesn't have much else in her life, poor gal. Just her job as a dental assistant. No boyfriend or nothing. She ain't what you'd call a looker . . . sort of mousy. But she's real nice. I'd ask her on a date, but she doesn't do much for me in the you-know-what department. Still, I don't mind talking with her when we bump into each other.

The three-decker where we live in Dorchester has no parking, so if you have a car you need to rent a place somewhere else or take your chances on the street. You can get a residential sticker, but in the winter when it snows, you have to get any parked car out of the way of the plows. And that can be a real pain in the ass. I don't think Mildred has thought much about that, but she better because it's already October and the shit's sure coming. Of course, she could park that toy on the sidewalk and nobody would probably notice.

Mildred lives in the rear flat on the floor above me. She says she moved here right out of school a dozen years ago. I was in her place for coffee for the first time a couple months back. It's real tiny. Think she's got two rooms, but she made it look homey. Some of the paintings on her walls are kind of screwy. Looks like someone just threw cans of paint at them. She says they're called Abstracts. Whatever they are, they don't do nothing for me.

She also had this coffee maker contraption that makes just one cup at a time and in all different flavors. Don't understand how people are into all those silly candy-tasting coffees. To me a cup of Joe should be a cup of Joe, plain and simple. That's the way I look at it. Guys at work make fun of all that fancy sounding coffee they have at Starbucks that costs more than a down payment on a house.

Mildred invited me for a ride in her car tomorrow, and I said okay. Didn't have anything better to do. Hope she ain't getting any ideas about us being more than just friends. Like I said, she ain't really my type. Besides I have a good 20 years on her. She says she wants to drive down to Plymouth to see that Pilgrim rock there. Seen it once when I was a kid. No big deal. Looks like any other rock you come across. Think they just picked any rock and claimed it was the one the Pilgrims saw when they landed. But it'll be nice to get out of town for a few hours. She just better not make any moves, because I'd have to set her straight.

* * *

We planned to go for our ride after catching coffee at DDs. When she showed up at my door, she had the biggest smile on her face. Like a kid ready to go for ice cream. Kind of tickled me. But that big smile of hers was gone as soon as she noticed someone had gone and keyed her brand new car. She looked like someone had kicked her in the gut.

"I don't believe it," she said, getting all teary eyed.

53

It was a long scratch running from the tail light to the headlight. Looked like a long ugly slash on something that had been pretty.

"Why would anybody do such a cruel thing, Hank? People can be so nasty."

"It can be fixed. *I* can fix it," I offered.

"I have insurance, but the deductible is five-hundred dollars, and I can't afford that after spending everything I had to buy my car."

"Look, to heck with going to Plymouth. I'll get some touch up paint at Benny's and take care of it, okay, Mildred?"

"Oh, I just remembered that the car came with a tube of touch up. It's in the glove compartment."

"Well, there you go. We're in like Flynn. Why don't you go down to Dunkin' and get us some Joe and donuts—jelly for me. I'll get to work."

"Really. You'll do this for me?"

"Hey, what are *friends* for?"

"Thank you, Hank. I really appreciate it. You're so nice," she said, touching my arm.

I found the tube of touch up and began to put it on the scratch, which wasn't too deep. Before I was halfway through, Mildred returned with breakfast.

"Oh my God, it looks great! I can hardly see where the scratch was."

"Not done yet, but it pretty much does the trick. Good thing you had touch up from the dealer. It was a perfect match. When you buy car paint at a store, it never really blends in."

"Hey, Hank, we still have time for our drive, if you want" said Mildred, her mood becoming jolly.

"Sure . . . why not. Day's still young," I replied.

In a half hour, we were on our way down to Plymouth, and all seemed right with the world for Mildred as she hummed along with the car radio. Along the way, she started asking questions about my kids from my marriage—a girl and a boy nearly grown up who live with their mother and her second husband in Revere. I had mentioned having kids to Mildred a while back, but didn't say nothing more about them. Because I don't like getting personal with people, even someone like Mildred.

"They're good kids," I answered and turned the talk back to her.

"How come you haven't got yourself a husband?"

"Never found a guy who wanted to go there. I mean I once had a relationship that lasted almost a year. But then we just stopped seeing each other. I think he found someone else. It's okay. I don't know that I want to get married anyway. Guess I would if Mr. Perfect showed up, but what's the chance of that happening?" said Mildred, with a self-conscious giggle.

Our trip to Plymouth turned out to be fun, and I agreed to go for a ride with her up to Salem sometime to check out all that witch stuff. Even though her car was smaller than most, it rode just fine, and it wasn't all that cramped inside. I don't have a car anymore. Seems a waste of money when you live in the city. Mildred never owned a car, so she just felt the need. Wants to take lots of sightseeing trips around New England, since she's originally from Delaware, so it made sense to her to save up and buy a vehicle.

* * *

It wasn't a week after our day in Plymouth when I woke up to loud screams outside my apartment window. When I checked them out, I couldn't believe what I was seeing. Mildred was whacking at a guy with a baseball bat and had him pretty much pinned to the ground next to her car. I threw my clothes on as fast as I could in order to get out there before she did the guy in. By the time I reached the street, the cops were already there and they were putting Mildred in one police car and the young dude in another. I gave her a "what's going on look," and she just shook her head like she was in shock, which made me feel real sorry for her. Then the cop behind the wheel told me to step away from the car.

"What happened officer? Why you arresting Mildred?"

"Taking both of them in to sort this out. Both have a story. She attacked the young man with a bat. He's kind of messed up, but nothing fatal."

Before I could ask anything further, both squad cars pulled away.

She attacked the young man with a bat. The cop's words echoed in my head. *What the hell for*, I wondered, and then I saw the likely reason. Her car had been keyed again. *Jeez, never thought she had that kind of brass in her. Good for you, Mildred. Got to admire a person who stands up for themself. Most chicks would just rollover in that situation. You got some big ones, honey.*

As soon as I got myself together, I headed to the police station to see what was going down. Just as I entered the doors of the local precinct, I spotted Mildred in the lobby.

"They let you go?" I asked.

"I told them what happened. That I saw him keying my car, and when I told him to stop or I'd hit him with my bat, he swore at me. I don't care to repeat what he called me, but it really set me off, so I gave him a good whack. They said he had a long criminal record, and so let me go. He's being charged with malicious destruction of personal property. I might be charged with hitting that loser, but I don't care."

There was something about the flush in her cheeks as she spoke that gave her face a prettiness I'd never noticed before. At that moment, she looked different—better—to me. I began to figure maybe I'd never really seen her the right way.

"Come on, Mildred. Let's go get a coffee at Dunkin. It's on me. Maybe we could take that ride up to Salem this weekend?"

"You're such a sweet man, Hank," she said, and I gave her a long hug.

#

After

He's deeply disturbed but has concealed that fact well enough to keep from drawing unwanted attention. He wonders what it is that has him clenching his fists and feeling the rise of his heartbeat? Is it the sudden darkness in the room or the icy air that seeps through a break in the windowpane that makes him so jumpy? He smells something, too, which puts him off . . . churns his stomach. A scent that rose from the freshly severed arm of an Afghan villager he rushed to aid as an army medic. Then there's the rose-colored water that trickles onto his shoes as he slumps at the basin's edge. *Clare*, he thinks, *you shouldn't have done it.* His lover's hand twitches in a postmortem spasm and he screams for her out of habit.

#

Fast Fool

Beware the fury of a [in]patient man.
   —John Dryden

Once I lost it and went way over the line letting my temper get the best of me. Hey, I'll admit I have a short fuse, but on that particular occasion, I really just let it rip. Sure, I was drag-ass tired after a day shadowing this broad who was cheating on her old man, but that's no excuse for putting myself in a potentially bad situation. An assault charge and my PI license is a goner . . . and so am I, for that matter. Not a damn other thing I can do to make a living. No other skills, period. Suppose I grew up dumb on that score, but it's not been so bad. Got plenty of freedom, if not a lot of dough.

Anyway, here's what happened. I was on my way back to my pad, and I stopped at this White Castle on Langley for burgers . . . love those quarter size heartburns. So the joint was empty at 2 AM, except for this black dude waiting at the takeout counter. I took my place next to him and waited for service. Finally, this young Latino comes out from the back and begins cleaning the grill, totally ignoring us.

Well, me and this other customer just stood there figuring the guy would stop what he was doing and take our order. Wrong. He just kept scraping at the frigging grill like we weren't even there. The black cat looked at me and rolled his eyes, and I did the same back. Still, we didn't say or do anything, but I could feel my blood pressure beginning to rise. *Is this patty flipper deaf, dumb, and blind?* I wondered, and cleared my throat loud enough to be heard a block away.

Okay, still nothing. Now I realize he's making some kind of 'fuck you' statement, and I'm not having it any longer. I consider hopping over the counter and whacking him in his greasy noggin, but then I come up with another idea. I grab hold of a squeezable mustard container and fling it at him like I'm Roger Clemens. Threw it hard as a son of a bitch. And, man, to my supreme delight it lands on his head and bursts open, splattering its yellow contents all over him.

He's totally shocked by my fast ball and just stands there not believing what's just happened to him. The black dude standing next to me looks astonished, too, and then he smiles and gives me a high five. Now I know it's time to get the frig out of there to avoid some real shit flying, like the taco head calling the cops or something. So I hightail it from the place, and jump into my car. By the time I pull away, the refried is coming out of the door and yelling at me. I gun it and fly past him, giving him the benefit of my middle finger.

On my drive home, I can't stop laughing at what just happened—about how the mustard bottle landed so perfectly on the stupid prick's head. "Jesus," I mumble to myself as I reach my digs, "It just popped open and covered him. How freaking great was that? Asshole didn't get hurt either. That's good, but he got the point. Damn right, he did. Wonder if he'll pull that shit attitude on customers anymore?"

In the back of my mind, a little voice warns me that he may have gotten my plate number, but I just don't give one shit if he did or didn't. I'm feeling too high about everything at the moment. Besides, there's no way the other customer there would give me up for that wetback, I tell myself. He was as pissed as I was, and if I'm any judge of character, he was about to tear that burrito's head off, too.

Still, I have a hard time getting to sleep, because I can't stop thinking about those tasty White Castle burgers I didn't get. Maybe I'll go back tomorrow and get some and see if that enchilada got the mustard out of his dew rag.

* * *

The next day I go back to the White Castle because I still have this major craving for their bitsy burgers. I'm curious, too, if the Rican, or whatever he is, is there. I know I could get in trouble if he remembers me, but I do crap like this. I got a self-destructive side to me that's come close to doing me in a couple of times. Can't explain what it is. Maybe got it from my old man. He tried to off himself in a couple of times, but finally was done in by his three-pack a day habit.

So sure as hell when I get there, who's behind the counter still working the grill? Yup, it's him. No shit. I take a seat at the counter, and he immediately takes my order. *What the . . .! You don't recognize me? What's with the good service, too?* I wonder, and I order a half-dozen of their artery cloggers and a cup of Joe. Damned if he doesn't thank me with a wide smile. *Yeah, what the . . .?*

I gulp down my food and get ready to leave. As soon as I rise from my stool, a cop stops me and asks if I was in the place the night before. I play dumb. Then he tells me an employee says I attacked him.

"No way," I say, and show him my detective permit.

"Oh, yeah," he says, "I heard of you. Guys at the station say you're a standup guy. Helped them solve a couple cases."

"Yeah," I say. That was me."

The cop calls the White Castle loser over and questions him. "So you say he hit you with something? What *something* was that?"

"Mustard. He hit me with a mustard container, and it got all over me."

"French's?"

"Huh? No, Gulden's."

The cop turns back to me and says he's got to take me in, because attacking someone with Gulden's instead of French's mustard is a felony.

The lowrider and me look at each other with a "you got to be kidding me" expression on our mugs.

"C'mon," the cop says, grabbing me by the arm, and then he lets go and starts laughing like a hyena. "Leave a tip to cover his dry cleaning," he says, pointing to the mule.

When the flatfoot's gone, I put a fiver on the counter to pay for my food.

"Keep the change," I say, and begin to leave.

"Hey, this ain't gonna cover the cost of cleaning my uniform, man," says the nacho, waving his spatula threateningly.

This gets my goat, and I reach for the ketchup container this time.

#

Slow Transit

I don't like traveling, period. I like being at
places and I like going to places, but I don't
like forms of transportation.
—Travis Barker

I was aerating the soil in my garden in preparation for installing some tulip bulbs for the coming spring when my trowel struck something hard. To my surprise, the buried object turned out to be quite long and wide. After considerable excavation, I realized it was a door. *How could that be?* I wondered, since I had planted flowers in that very spot the year before and had found nothing.

When I had finally cleared the soil away from the secreted portal, I pulled at its brass handle and it creaked opened. I had barely lifted it more than a few inches when a gloved hand curled around its edge and pushed hard enough to knock me off my feet. Terror seized me and I screamed at whatever it was that was slowly emerging from what apparently was some kind of underground chamber. Strange metallic squealing sounds emanating from it added to my dismay.

"Excuse me," said a proper-looking gentleman, shaking the dirt from his double-breasted wool frock and bowler. "Is this Chesham Station? I've been on the bloody Tube for what seems a century?"

#

The Bequest

You can tell a lot about a person from his underwear.
                                    —Rachel Bilson

When a lifelong friend of mine died, his mother thought to give me some of what she called his "good" clothes. When I resisted her offer, she protested, saying that it was ridiculous to let them go to waste since they were practically brand new and Brandon and I were about the same size. The idea still didn't sit well with me. It seemed kind of creepy, but I realized it was a gesture of kindness on her part, because I'd been a close pal of her son since we'd both been in elementary school.

A week after Brandon's funeral, Mrs. Gibson called and told me to come by her house because she had a large box of his things that she was sure I could use. I told her I'd be by when I could, but I planned to avoid doing so for as long as possible, hoping she would loose track and forget about it. It wasn't until my girlfriend, Hannah, got on my case that I made plans to pick up the stuff.

"Okay, but I'm going to give it to Goodwill as soon as I can," I grumbled.

"That's fine with me, because I sure don't want you walking around with Brandon's clothes on. Yuk! That would be just too spooky."

The next day I went to Mrs. Gilson's house, and she seemed thrilled to see me, although it was evident that she'd been crying.

"It was very hard going through Brandon's stuff. Everything I touched brought back memories, but I'm really glad you want some of his clothes. He liked expensive shirts, and he had some real nice slacks, too. There's a bunch of other things in the box I thought you could use. Now, please don't be a stranger, Mitch. Just seeing you makes it seem like he's still with us."

I promised her I would visit when I could and returned home with the heavy carton of unwanted items. My plan was to take it to the local Goodwill drop box on my way to work after the weekend.

"Let's see what's in there," said Hannah.

"Really, why?"

"Just curious," she replied, heading out to my car where I'd left the box.

"Let the guy rest. He wouldn't want us going through his clothes. Would you want people going through your personal things after you died?" I asked.

By the time I reached Hannah, she had already opened my car's hatchback door and the lid to the box.

"Oh, look," she said, as I approached her. "Undies."

"Wha . . .?"

"Tighty whities? That surprises me. I took Brandon to be more the boxer type."

"Mrs. Gibson gave me his underwear?"

"I think they've been worn. Although they're perfectly clean. No stains or anything. She ironed them, too."

"That's gross. His *used* underwear? Jesus! Why would she give them to me?"

"She's in mourning and not thinking right. Don't get so upset, hon."

"Brandon's got to be turning over in his grave. That's it. Close the box. I'm taking it to the Goodwill drop box right now."

"There's a bunch of his used T's in here, too," said Hannah, digging deeper into the carton.

"Enough already! Just close the box, and let me take it, okay?"

"Oh, my God!"

"What?"

"Look at this."

Just as Hannah lifted an object from the depths of the box, I saw a bright flash and felt excruciating pain in the side of my head. Then everything went dark. I'm told it was three days later that I regained consciousness in the hospital. Apparently, Mrs. Gibson had packed her son's target practice pistol in with his clothes, and it went off accidentally when Hannah was about to show it to me.

The police investigated the incident but concluded that it was just one of those bizarre near tragedies where no one was really to blame. Of course, Hannah felt horrible, as did Mrs. Gibson, who visited me daily until I was discharged from the hospital.

When I asked her why she put Brandon's gun in the box, she said she didn't want it around her house and thought I'd like it because she recalled us loving to play with our toy guns when we were kids.

Though I never did ask Mrs. Gibson why she gave me her son's slightly used underwear, it was apparent to me that Brandon was dead set against my wearing them.

#

Two Old Cops Arguing

One says to the other . . .

"We were close friends. I never thought you'd do what you did."

"Obviously I never should have told you. I thought after all these years . . ."

"What? That I'd be less upset? That I would have come to terms with it?"

"It's been over three decades. I'm really surprised you still feel so strongly about it."

"Of course, I still feel *strongly* about it. It was very important to me."

"Wow, I guess it was. I'm amazed. I never thought you'd react this way."

"That's because you lack the ability to feel guilt."

"Look, what do you want me to do, for God's sake?"

"If I have to tell you, then it's not worth the bother."

"So you think what I did was *that* terrible?"

"Damn right, it was *that* terrible."

"C'mon. We all experience temptation. It was just a . . ."

"Just a . . . *what?*"

"Hey, no one's perfect. Are you?"

"It doesn't have to do with being *perfect*. It has to do with honor and integrity."

"Can't you just put it behind you once and for all?"

"Easier said than done, pal."

"All this because of a silly . . .?"

"What if I'd done it to you? How would you feel?"

"Not as freaked out as you are about it. "

"Of course not. I have a conscience. You clearly lack one."

"Stop! I give up. I'm a terrible person. How can I make amends?"

"At the very least, you might show some remorse."

"You want me to show *remorse*?"

"Yes, that's what I'd *like* you to do."

"Okay . . . *okay*! I'm sorry I took the last doughnut."

"You could say it with *more* feeling."

"Stay put while I get my service revolver."

#

Riding the Serpent

I thought a stick was a snake. Until it bit me, and then I knew.
                                                        —Jarod Klinz

The snake seemed as long as the dirt road was wide. The rutted strip led to our base located at the edge of the Everglades. We were coming back after a ride in Floyd's powder blue 1962 Chevy Impala convertible that he'd bought with his re-up money. He had never owned a car as new and cool as the Chevy, and he sat in the driver's seat like a king on his thrown.

"Will you look at this bad ass baby? Ain't she some kind of beauty?" he gushed repeatedly. "Two years old, but she look brand spankin' new."

We all enthusiastically agreed, and I wondered what it must look like to people as we moved through the streets of tiny Carol City, Florida, just a couple miles from the army missile site where we were all stationed. By some of the curious looks we got, I figured folk must have thought that Bob, Roddy, and me were being driven by a chauffer because Floyd was colored.

"Yes sir . . . damn sure better than my '53 Ford. Car only had two gears when I give it to my lil' brother after I signed up. He could only get it going to 10 miles an hour. That was enough for him, 'cause he was just 12. Pretty soon it could only go in reverse, but he drove it that way. Got in trouble when he backed it all the way into town, so he's ridin' his bike again."

"They let kids that age drive in Georgia?" asked Bob. "I didn't get behind the wheel 'til I was 14. Tennessee got tougher laws than Georgia, I guess."

"Seems so," said Floyd, with a bright toothy grin. "Look here now. We riding in one sweet ass beauty . . . ain't we boys?"

"Yeah, man, one sweet ass beauty," I echoed.

Unlike Floyd, Bob had a mouthful of rotting teeth, which gave him the worst breath I'd ever smelled. I usually managed to stand far enough away from him to keep from being hit by it, but this time I was sitting next to him in the back seat of the car.

"You got to be 15 and a half to drive in West Virginia. And then it's only a learner's permit," chimed in Roddy, who sat next to Floyd in the front. "I didn't get a license until I was 21 and got money enough to buy my own car."

"Did they have special pedals so your feet could reach them?" cracked Bob.

Roddy was no more than five foot four, if that, and he was constantly ribbed because of his shortness. He seemed to take it in good stride, but I sensed it bothered him more than he showed. It was Roddy who first spotted the snake.

"Holy crap! What the . . .? Look at that goddamn thing!" he blurted, pointing ahead.

"Oh, lordy!" gasped Floyd, hitting the brakes.

But he was too late and the car ran right over it.

"Well, that's one dead snake," I said, as we all turned around expecting to see a flattened carcass.

But there was no snake to be seen. "Where the heck is it? It ain't there," said Floyd, panic rising in his voice.

"Maybe it got away. They move fast when they got to," observed Roddy.

"Could be it climbed under the car," I said, not anticipating the consequences of my remark.

"Shit!" bellowed Floyd, hitting the accelerator.

"That mother could come right up inside the car, man," shouted Bob, and we all lifted our legs onto the seats.

The last mile to the base was covered in record time, although the large ruts in the road nearly caused us to be thrown from the convertible. As soon as we reached the parking lot, we all jumped out of Floyd's prized ride without even opening the doors.

"Aren't you going to put the top up?" I asked Floyd, who now stood further away from the car than any of us.

"No damn way I'm goin' near that thing 'til that snake is gone for sure."

"But it's going to rain. You know how it is this time of year. Clouds open up like waterfalls. That Chevy of yours will fill up like a tub," said Roddy.

"Don't care. As long as that snake is in there, you ain't gonna' find ol' Floyd near it."

"I bet it's not under it," I offered, trying to coax Floyd into putting up the cover. "I mean, how could it jump under it when we were traveling so fast, anyway? Probably got flung away by the back wheels and ended up in the brush."

"I heard about snakes getting under cars when people ran over them," said Bob, and I gave him a fierce 'shut up' look.

"I think it would be pretty impossible for a snake that size to just disappear under your car that quickly, man," I pressed.

Trying to get back in my good graces, Bob added, "Yeah, Floyd, he'd have to have super powers to move that fast."

"That's what I'm afraid of. He's some kind of a monster serpent. Maybe mix of alligator and python. Forget that, man. I'm going to my tent and get some rest," said Floyd, moving toward the entrance to the base.

"Someone should put the top up," I said, but when both Bob and Roddy remarked that they wouldn't go near the convertible in case the snake was still there, I figured to leave it alone as well

As we headed to our respective billets, we joked about how Floyd looked as white as we were when he thought the snake was somewhere under his new car.

"Didn't think colored guys could turn pale," observed Roddy, "but Floyd looked like a ghost."

* * *

Four days later, after nearly continuous downpours, Floyd's car remained right where he'd parked it—and with the top still down.

"He says he might check on it tomorrow. The inside must be ruined by now. Too bad, it was such great looking wheels," said Bob.

"A fish tank now, I bet," added Roddy.

"Yeah, that poor guy has a messed up car and three more years in the army to show for it," said Bob.

Actually, Floyd had more to show for his time in the military than a damaged car. He had dropped out of school in the 9th grade but had managed to get his high school equivalency diploma while serving in Korea. He was a corporal and would probably make the rank of buck sergeant during his new enlistment. In the end, not bad for a colored guy from a backwater town in southern Georgia, I thought.

"It'll dry out. Seats might be a little soggy at first, but it should be basically okay," I commented.

"That snake might still be in it," remarked Roddy.

"It probably drowned if it was," said Bob.

"The sun's out. Let's go check it out," I suggested.

The three of us approached the car cautiously. First we checked its underside from a safe distance in case there was any sign of the snake. We then looked inside and were surprised when it didn't resemble a water trough. The rainwater must have drained out, we concluded.

"Careful, it might be coiled up under the seats," said Bob, as we stood scanning the convertible's interior.

With considerable trepidation, we opened the car's doors fully expecting the snake to slither out at any moment.

"It ain't in there," observed Roddy. "Let's go tell Floyd."

Despite informing him that his car appeared free of unwanted life forms, it still took a heap of convincing to get him back near it. When he finally gave in and went with us to the parking lot, it took him a good 5 minutes to get close to the opened doors. It was another 10 minutes of hesitation and reckoning before he dared sit in the driver's seat.

"Shit, my ass be all wet," he complained, slowly wrapping his large black hands around the steering wheel

"What'd you expect? It's been out here in the rain for days," said Roddy.

"Guess I'll take it down to the gas station and get it on the lift to make sure that snake still ain't underneath," said Floyd, cranking the engine. "Listen to that, will you? Least the rain didn't mess up the motor. She purring like a kitten."

"Good luck," I said. "Hope the snake doesn't drop on the mechanic's head."

"Well, if it drop on anyone's head, it gonna' be his, not mine. Ain't gettin' under there, I'll tell you."

"Good move," said Bob.

"C'mon, guys. Get in. Come with me," said Floyd.

We declined his invitation and watched as Floyd started down the dirt road toward town on his own. He was only about a hundred yards away when we heard him scream and saw him jump from the car. It continued on without him and veered to the right, disappearing over an embankment.

"What the *hell* . . .?" yelled Roddy, as we ran toward where Floyd was standing.

"What happened?" I asked when we reached him.

"It was under my seat and stuck its head up 'tween my legs. Thought it was gonna' chew off my balls," replied Floyd, truly shaken.

"Holy shit," said Bob. "Let's go see where the car ended up."

Floyd refused to venture anywhere near the brush and stayed back by the road as we went in search of his runaway Chevy.

"It's in the canal," reported Bob, who had run ahead of us.

Sure enough, half of the car was submerged in the narrow waterway.

"Well, that killed it. Shot now with the motor in the water like that," said Roddy. "Not worth a shit no more."

When we informed Floyd of the fate of his beloved vehicle, he smiled and appeared to breath a sigh of relief.

"Bet that ol' snake got his comeuppance."

"But what about your new car?" I asked. "You can get it towed out of the canal. Maybe it can be saved . . ."

"No, I'll let it stay right where it be. Heck, I'll reenlist in 3 years and get me another."

On our walk back to the base, we all began to laugh at what had happened . . . and ol' Floyd laughed the loudest.

#

Marital Abyss

It comes to me during another sleepless night following an all too frequent torrent of accusations and invectives: *Her thought process is* wrong. She doesn't see that her direction leads away from reason. I can't do a thing about it, although I've tried. So I deal with her dark mood up to a point. That is, until it becomes too much for me to handle. Then I vent my frustration, which only deepens her iron resolve to be miserable . . . and to make me the same.

#

Like a . . .

(Repeat the title before each item below)

Bird with one wing . . .
Rock in transition . . .
Wet and humid desert . . .
Triangle with four sides . . .
Dysfunctional functionary . . .
Generous miser . . .
New car with rust . . .
Satisfied cynic . . .
Planned accident . . .
Bible missing Genesis . . .
Healthy cigarette . . .
Pageless book . . .
Good time in ICU . . .
Nun at a disco . . .
Single crutch . . .
Bestseller no one bought . . .
Nap while sleeping . . .
Wedding with no vows . . .
Deaf telephone operator . . .
Shadow and no surface . . .
Ghost against haunting . . .
Wave that doesn't roll . . .
Shrill Stradivarius . . .
Gentle hurricane . . .
Bumper and no fender . . .
One-armed octopus . . .
Keyboard sans screen . . .
Missile and no enemy . . .
Motionless mobile . . .
Silent thunderstorm . . .
Flawed masterpiece . . .
Rose missing petals . . .
One channel television . . .

Palm tree in Alaska . . .
Killer and no victim . . .
Lawn without soil . . .
Bloodless hemorrhage . . .
Child who won't play . . .
Bell with no chime . . .
Dieting glutton . . .
Talkative monk . . .
Slow cheetah . . .
Peaceful war . . .
Compassionate hater . . .
Legless centipede . . .
Disease that cares . . .
Cat with eight lives . . .
List with no purpose . . .

#

Burying Yourself

What you wear to the grave is always safe from criticism.
　　　　　　　　　　　　　　—Sander Howling

Alison asked her 81 year-old spouse what clothes he wanted to wear at his wake.

"Huh? That's a weird thing to say. Why the heck are you asking me that? Do you know something I don't," he responded, slightly taken aback.

"I don't know. It just seems like a reasonable question to ask because appearance is so important to you."

"Well, I'm perfectly healthy, so it isn't something I've given much thought."

"Yes, it was a silly question. I was just thinking about what I'd like to be buried in, so I figured I'd ask you."

"Jeez, Alison, you're 14 years younger than me. Why would you even be thinking about that?"

"This morning I was standing in my closet and looking at my outfits, and the thought just came to me out of the blue. Sorry, it's ridiculous."

"Well, now that you mention it . . ."

"Forget it, darling. You know me. Sometimes I say things without thinking. Didn't mean to upset you."

"Actually, I'd like to be laid out in my blue Armani suit with my Stefani Ricci dress shirt and my Charvet silk tie."

"Really, what about the tie I gave you for your last birthday? I had it specially made from one of my designs."

"Well, I don't think it's the right tie to be laid to rest in, sweetheart. The look isn't appropriate for such a serious occasion. It should be worn when we go to a . . . costume party."

"A *costume party?* That's what you think of my art work?"

"I didn't mean it that way . . ."

"Well, what *way* did you mean it?"

"I meant it's kind of . . . *well,* a bit . . ."

"Do you have any idea how long it took me to create that unusual design, and you're saying it looks . . ."

"*Unusual,* like you say. Maybe a little *too* . . ."

"Too *what?* Just what are you getting at, Herb? Are you saying it's too *ugly,* too *silly,* too *tasteless* . . .?"

"No . . . no, I'm getting my words all mixed up. Actually, I think it's the perfect looking tie to be buried in."

"Now that's a heck of a thing to say about what I've put so much of my creative energy into. It should be *buried,* huh?""

"I'm not feeling very well, honey."

"Good, I'll get you the tie."

#

Nothing Bothers Me

Nothingness not being nothing, nothingness being emptiness.
                    —Isabelle Adjani

I've been pondering my end since I reached 60, and I'm several years closer to it now. It's hard for me to embrace the notion that sooner than later I'll succumb to nothing. Not being a religious man, I see no alternative to the Big Empty, as my friend sometimes refers to it. I'll simply no longer *be*— game over, offline forever. The only upside to this is that I won't know it, because how can you know or experience nothingness? What gets me is facing nothing when I'm still something and know I'll soon be nothing. That scares the shit out of me, even though I'm told there's nothing to fear. The problem is how does one overcome one's fear of nothing? I see the prospect of nothing as something I have to live with until I have nothing left to live. This fixation on nothing won't end until my awareness of nothing ceases to be and I'm *not* to be anymore. Yes, *to be or not to be* is *the question.* There are times I'm so frightened of nothing that I feel doing myself in is the only way to overcome my fear of it. But then I'm so afraid of nothing that I can't end the little something I have remaining. The other day my therapist asked what was disturbing me because I've been so depressed lately. She was puzzled when I told her that *nothing* was bothering me.

#

82

Parking Violation

Revenge always begins with craziness and ends in shame.
　　　　　　　　　　　　—Author unknown

One of Glen Wheeler's favorite pastimes was sitting on a bench in Gaylord Common in the early evening and taking in its lovely flora and fauna. The park also provided him with some amusement as he watched the city's derelicts gather before they headed to the nearby homeless shelter on Calvert Street for the night. During warm weather many would elect to remain outside sharing their cheap wine with one another––if anyone had some to share. The cops seldom disturbed them and when their booze ran out most would stake out a bench or a piece of lawn to curl up on until dawn.

Glen tried to imagine what caused these men to end up as vagrants and outcasts. And a bit of his heart went out to them. On a few occasions, he gave them money but was forced to stop this practice after they accosted him for handouts as soon as he appeared on the Common. The destitute and once passive men became hostile when he refused them a handout.

Finally the situation got to the point where the panhandlers would harass him with nasty names. On two occasions, they'd even tossed their empty bottles at him. This forced Glen to avoid the public grounds altogether, which made him resentful, too. Spending time in the park had been the highlight of his day and their belligerent behavior forced him to search elsewhere to spend his leisure time. But no place came close to the bucolic setting of the city's primary green space.

* * *

Glen grew more and more angry with the drunkards who denied him the pleasure he'd once derived in the sprawling natural oasis. *They should be run out of there. Why should these lowlife keep respectable citizens like me from enjoying what my taxes help pay for? These social rejects contribute nothing. Something should be done,* he thought, contemplating possible measures to regain what he had lost. It had been a long time since his anger had raised its ugly head. In the past that anger had gotten him into trouble and once resulted in a brief time in jail.

After obsessing over the frustrating situation for several days, a possible solution finally occurred to him. While the bums were sleeping, he would douse them with gasoline and set them on fire. *That will take care of the problem once and for all. The place will be mine again.*

When Glen arrived at the park long after midnight intent on executing his plan, he was baffled by what he encountered.

"Where are they? There's no one here. Dammit!" he growled, not realizing the irony of his lament.

He sat in his once favorite spot and waited in the hope the usual troupe of reprobates would reappear. Sleep finally overtook him, and not long afterwards one of his intended victims quietly relieved Glen of both his wallet and container of propellant.

* * *

"Hey you, get up! Move on! No more sleeping it off in the park. Can't do that any more. New law passed against that," growled a voice that pulled Glen from a deep sleep.

"Huh, a *new* law? When? That's great . . ."

"Let me see some identification," demanded a uniformed officer.

"Okay. I was going to . . . I mean I came here to . . ." muttered Glen digging through his pockets.

"Well, where's your ID, buddy? I'm waiting."

"It's gone. I had it when I came. Someone must have . . ."

"Sure, you were robbed, right? Now you're coming with me. No ID and I've got to take you in."

"No, wait. I had it when I got here, and my gas can . . ."

"Your what?"

"Nothing . . . *nothing*. I just had a package, and it's missing, too."

The policeman took Glen by the arm and marched him away. As he was led through the park, he caught sight of some of the homeless men he'd planned to immolate. Each held a brown bag that clearly contained a liquor bottle.

"Some of your friends?" asked the officer, with a smirk.

\#

Not Ready for Prime Time

The renowned American poet Brendan Galvin said that he had to write for 15 years before he knew what he was doing. I think, *oh shit, if that's the case, I've got 8 more years to go! What about all the work I've published over the past 7 years during a frenzy of creativity? Will I come to recognize that it's all flawed in some way because of my impetuous pen? Will I then despise what I've written and wish that it would all vanish to spare me embarrassment and ridicule? How can one make something disappear once it's been relegated to print and covers? Was I too quick to seek an audience? Should I have kept it to myself? Placed it in a sealed file and tucked it away until the time arrived when I could better recognize my deficiencies . . . until Galvin said I would know what I was doing?*

#

Personal Development

Start with big dreams and make life worth living.
—Stephen Richards

In late spring the Austrian Autobahn Authority set to work clearing away the buildings that once constituted the Mitterwallner's dairy farm. A road connecting Mulau to Straublin was finally to be built after many delays. Consequently, a dozen private residences along the projected route were to be razed to accommodate the new motorway. Despite what was considered to be generous compensation by the government, several property owners fought the plan. After years of frustrating court battles, however, the farmers were forced to sell.

Autobahn engineer Max Prock was charged with removing all buildings that stood in the way of the planned four-lane freeway between the two towns. Before giving the go-ahead to demolition crews, he had to inspect targeted structures to make certain everything of value (copper pipes, brass fittings . . .) was stripped from them and that any inadvertently overlooked personal items were returned to families that once owned the buildings.

Two days after signing off on the Mitterwallner property, Prock was contacted by the   demolition crew chief and told that something of interest had been discovered in a hidden subfloor of the dairy's barn.

"I've just begun holiday with my wife and children," snapped Prock. "What would you have me do, Waldheim?"

"We can't go forward with our work, Max, since what we've found are clearly the valuables of the prior owner. You know the rules when such discoveries are made? Should we go on to the next property?"

"*Scheisse!*" spit Prock. "I'll be there in the morning. Do nothing until I arrive."

Prock's wife, Hilda, understandably baulked when he told her that he had to return to the worksite. The demands of his job had become a point of tension, and Max knew that his devotion to his job was having a negative impact on their relationship.

"Please don't make this harder than it is, Hilda. Do you think I like being pulled away from my family on holiday? I promise I'll return quickly."

"Fine," said Hilda, dismissively. "The children and I will amuse ourselves as we usually do."

Shortly after sunrise, Prock put a few things into his valise and filled the gas tank of his Opel Astra for the drive to the Mulau-Straublin worksite. In three-hours, he arrived and his mood had further deteriorated. *This job is ruining everything*, he grumbled, as he hurried into the construction trailer. There he was greeted by Waldheim.

"Sorry, Max. I know you were on holiday with the family, but this is a very puzzling situation. What we found beneath the barn is really quite amazing."

"Well, what is it that's so important that I had to abandon my wife and children?"

"Original oil paintings."

"Huh . . . *paintings?*"

"Yes, let me show you. We haven't touched a thing."

Prock and Waldheim walked to where the barn had stood until recently. What remained was a deep bunker with a vast chamber.

"There's a staircase at the back. Come let me show you. We can gain access to the underground room there," said Walheim.

They walked along a narrow corridor until they reached a large open area. Tarps covered several piles of objects.

"So let's have an unveiling," said Prock, and Waldheim quickly complied.

"I estimate there are easily 100 paintings here, and I think they were all done by the same person. An obvious master," remarked Waldheim.

"Have you contacted the Mitterwallners?"

"No, you said not to do anything until you got here."

"Well, I'll make the call. Get me their number."

After looking through the remaining paintings, they returned to the construction office, where Prock made the telephone call.

"Mr. Mitterwallner, this is Max Prock, chief engineer for the Autobahn, calling from your former property. We've discovered a large collection of paintings in what was a basement in your milking barn. We believe they must belong to you and would like you to come and claim them."

After a long silence, Christophe Mitterwallner responded with words that surprised Prock. "I know of no paintings, Mr.

Prock. If they are there as you say, someone else must have stored them there unbeknownst to my family."

"Well, since they are on your former property, they now belong to you by default, Mr. Mitterwallner."

"I . . . *we*, are not interested in them. Do with them as you please," replied Mitterwallner, who then abruptly hung up.

"*Gott . . . hilfe!*" grumbled Prock. "What now?"

"What's the matter"? asked Waldheim.

"The old man said they're not his paintings and they don't want them."

"That's odd. Well, we'll have to contact the Transportation Ministry, I suppose," said Waldheim.

"Yes, that would be the next thing to do," replied Prock, shaking his head in frustration.

Prock made the necessary call, and was told an official named Ludwig Bauer would arrive at the site in two days.

"*Verdammt!*" blurted Prock. "Now I'm stuck here until Bauer arrives. This is going to cause me big trouble on the home front."

He was all too correct as his wife said not to bother rejoining the family when he told her of his further delay.

"It will only disrupt things, Max, and I know you would rather stay at your job anyway, so that will make us all happy," she snarled, before abruptly ending what had been a brief, one-sided conversation.

As it turned out, the representative from the Transportation Ministry was a day late arriving, so Prock was left to brood about his bleak domestic situation even longer. When Ludwig Bauer finally showed up, Prock was barely communicative.

"Okay, we need a decision right away about these paintings to get this project back on track," he said, directing the just arrived official to the trench containing the canvasses.

After inspecting the paintings, Bauer informed Prock that he would have to bring in an art expert to evaluate them. At this Prock threw up his hands in exasperation and stomped away.

Three days later, a noted art historian from the University of Vienna spent the morning examining the colorful oil landscapes and still lifes. When he emerged from the dug out, he was ashen faced.

"Are you not well, Professor?" asked Bauer.

"Impossible! This is remarkable . . . unbelievable," he gasped.

"What are you saying?" asked Prock, his aggravation peaking. "Please tell us what you mean. We must get things moving here."

The elderly professor appeared on the verge of fainting and asked for a drink. Waldheim directed him to a seat and shouted to one of his workers to bring some water. It took the professor a while before he was able to gather himself.

"I cannot believe what I have seen. Those paintings down there are the work of . . ."

"Who?" growled Prock.

"Perhaps I shouldn't say. Maybe it's better not to say . . ."

"Tell us what you know. That's why we brought you here, Professor!" demanded Prock.

"There are major implications to this discovery. The world will be shocked. History will be rewritten," replied the professor, looking even paler than when he'd emerged from the underground vault.

"Tell us right now or we'll be forced to bring in another expert and withhold your fee," threatened Prock.

The professor stared blankly and mumbled to himself, "How could he have done these incredible paintings with everything he was doing . . . and to actually grow as an artist? Extraordinary! He was so mediocre when he started out. But how could he have produced all of this masterful work without anyone knowing? Nothing has ever been said or written. There is no record . . . "

"*Fick*, Professor! Please tell us *now!*" barked Prock, leaning into the professor's face.

"*In Ordnung . . . ja!*" answered the professor, emerging from his thoughts. "If you must know, I'll tell you. But understand that your troubles will only be starting."

"Fine. So what is this earth-shattering discovery?"

"The paintings down there are the work of . . ."

"*Yes, yes . . .?*" roared Prock.

"Hitler! They were all painted by *Adolf Hitler!*"

#

Three Times Under

The first time I pulled my way above the water's surface I saw the ferry moving away, and I screamed and waved my arms hoping to be rescued.

Help! Help!

The second time I broke the water's surface I saw a giant swell lifting toward the empty sky, and it blocked everything I had seen just seconds before.

Help! Hel . . .

The third time I groped my way beyond the water's surface I saw the shapeless light of the sun. *Why hadn't I learned to swim?* I reproached myself, the brightness giving way to the sea's dark interior.

Hel . . .

I'm gone . . . I'm gone. Three times under, I thought, but a wave miraculously carried me to the sandy shore. There I gasped for air as beach goers looked down at me with disdain.

And then I saw the sign:

"Private Beach"

Second Sentences

Writer Simon Bellamy asked a fellow scribe if he would contribute a follow up line to those listed in his message. He felt the sentences possessed a certain power and uniqueness worth cultivating, but he was suffering from a case of writer's block and unable to expand on them. Not long after he sent out his email request, he received the following suggestions (noted in *italics*):

Our heads are clogged with the detritus of human experience.

An ear cleansing solution and nasal decongestant purchased at his local pharmacy helped Ethan experience life from a clear perspective.

Fate had given Harry Donovan everything it had earmarked for him, and regrettably it had fallen short of his hopes and expectations.

Harry was miserable because he had yet to bowl a perfect 300.

The woman stared back at her severed legs as if looking into an aquarium tank filled with iridescent jellyfish.

Inexplicably, a peanut butter and jellyfish sandwich allowed her to continue jogging without her lower appendages.

Bella Consuela reached her hand into the sticky yellow place.

And kept it there until the police were forced to taze her.

Seymour found a way to illuminate the darkest corners of his mind.

By switching from a 40 to 100 watt light bulb.

You just don't get old; you feel others withering.

Heloise found a better place to rest her hand during intimacy with her elderly husband.

A fortune-teller told Wilma that it was in the past that she would find true happiness.

So she threw her car in reverse and ran over her ex-husband and his beautiful young fiancée.

And there she was . . . alone in the sultry innards of her Bahamas' hotel bedroom.

With her 3XL Plus Size baby doll negligee stretched to its absolute limits.

We're all molecules of energy passing through the wormhole of eternity.

So one really must watch one's caloric intake if one hopes to get to the other side.

How quick the body cools and stiffens.

That was the existential problem confronting Craig as he searched for the right dosage of Viagra.

Disappointed and irritated by what he felt were contrived—if not intentionally bogus—replies from his so-called colleague, Simon asked if he would provide him with an additional companion sentence. This one for the following:

He knew his dumb-ass writing cohort had far less talent than he did, so he wasn't surprised by his grossly inadequate contributions.

Simon no longer felt blocked.

#

That Deep Sweet Post-Coital Sleep

"It was so good, Johnny. It was the best ever. I've never felt like that before," she whispered moments before falling into a state of delicious unconsciousness.

To her delight, her lover awaited her in the dream that followed. His chest was exposed, revealing his sculpted pecks and broad shoulders. His muscles rippled and glistened in the bright moonlight and set her passions on fire . . . again.

"Take me," she said breathlessly. "Take me like never before."

And he did as she asked, pulling her into his strong arms and ravishing her short, stout body until every molecule of her being was rendered numb with pleasure.

"Oh, Johnny!" she cried in ecstasy, her arms tearing at his deeply tanned flesh. "Love me . . . love me hard and forever!"

When she awoke hours later, she discovered the page from the romance novel she'd been reading was missing . . . apparently ripped out of the paperback.

"Oh, no!" she exclaimed, "Another one of those love you and leave you types."

#

The Decision

Everybody is dealt a hand of cards. It's the way you choose to play them that matters.

—J. P. Carson

Gabe never forgot the thrill he experienced as a kid back in 1952 when he found a quarter on his way to school. Part of a poor family, that coin was a veritable fortune to him. He'd never had that much money of his own to spend as he wished, and his heart jumped as he wiped the dirt from the quarter and inspected it closely. The coin's date was the same as when he was born and this added to his excitement. His head swirled as he considered how he might spend it.

Lavoi's Drugs was on his route to school, and it was there that his friends bought their penny candy and packets of baseball cards. The prospect of owning a bunch of those cards caused Gabe to up his pace. Not only would his incredible windfall get him a dozen new cards for flipping, but they would also provide him with enough bubble gum to last for several days . . . that is, if he didn't share it with his sisters. *Maybe I'll give Sara and Judy one piece*, he thought, and then he changed his mind. *They wouldn't share any with me. They're so stingy.*

As Gabe approached the store, he clutched the precious quarter and dreamed of unwrapping a load of baseball cards with pictures of the game's greatest stars of the day. Every kid in the 1950s coveted cards with star players like Stan Musial, Yogi Berra, Warren Spahn, Joe DiMaggio, Willie Mays, and Ted Williams. Any one of these cards could be exchanged for ten or more regular cards. But the Ted Williams card was valued above all others in Gabe's hometown of Woonsocket, Rhode Island. To get a card with the Red Sox ace hitter was to strike the jackpot. It could bring as many as 20 cards in a trade.

The display of baseball cards was the focal point of the neighborhood boys who stopped at Lavoi's on their way to school, and Gabe was afraid that they might be picked through by the time he got there. The store had run out of the prized items more than once. However, to his relief, the stock of cards was plentiful. Moreover, just one kid was there before him, and after a couple of minutes, he left without making a purchase.

Gabe counted out an even dozen of the wrapped cards and was about to take them to the cash register when he was struck by a feeling of guilt about spending the quarter on himself. *I should give it to Mom for bread or something,* he considered. *She really needs it.*

But then he thought about the Ted Williams card he was sure would be found in the stack he held in his hand . . . and he came to his senses.

#

The Evening of a Solitary Senior

The elderly man sat on a park bench for hours watching children play and adults exercise their pets. At twilight he rose and slowly wandered back to his room above a former plumbing supply store. The stairs leading up to the second floor were rickety and the walls had large cracks causing loose plaster to form tiny powdery pyramids on the timeworn wooden risers. The decorated Korean War veteran opened the door to his room and flipped on the light switch. The dim bulb hanging from the ceiling revealed a single unmade bed, a bureau missing most of its knobs, and a metal table with a Formica top on which rested a two-burner hotplate, a handful of eating utensils, and a small pile of books. On the sill outside of the room's only window stood a half empty bottle of milk kept cool by the mid October air. The 81 year-old removed his jacket, sat next to the table, and lit a Camel. After he'd smoked it to a stub, he rose and went to the sink and filled a small pan, which he then placed on one of the hotplate's coils. While waiting for the water to boil, he opened one of his used paperbacks and began to read. His thick eyelids soon drooped and he nodded off—a thread of saliva dangled from his open mouth. The water in the pan had evaporated and the bottom of it was black and smoldering when he woke minutes later. The old man cursed loudly and grabbed at its handle with a soiled dishrag. He placed the scorched container in the sink and doused it with water. It sizzled loudly muffling his additional profanities. No one heard the senior citizen's clatter since he was the sole remaining tenant of the decrepit structure. His image in the cracked mirror over the sink held his attention while he refilled the pan with water. He remained vigilant until it boiled and then opened a soup packet, emptying its yellow contents into a cup. As he sipped his supper, he gazed with casual interest at a cockroach scampering from the rim of the sink to the small wastebasket beneath it. Wind rattled the feeble building while he smoked several more cigarettes and escaped deeper into the plot of his book. Eventually, he rose, removed his trousers, and slipped under the frayed bedspread. Sleep soon overtook him, causing his novel—*The Promised Land*—to slip from his hand and fall to the floor.

#

Friends In Crime

Right actions in the future are the best apologies
for bad actions in the past.
　　　　　　　　　　　—Tryon Edwards

For years we all met in the back of what was once Crowley's Garage on the edge of town to drink coffee and shoot the bull. There were five of us, and we'd arrive early morning and hang out until noon, when we'd finally head off in our respective directions. Since we were all retirees that generally meant heading home for lunch—and an afternoon nap.

These gatherings were an integral part of our lives, because they gave us an opportunity to share what occupied our thoughts—life's problems and pleasures, mostly the former. We often joked that our meetings were more bitch sessions than anything else. But if that's what they were, they served a valuable function. We could say things that would surely get us in trouble with our spouses and God knows who else.

It got so we spilled our guts about everything, even those things we thought we'd always keep locked away. It started when Frank Belton revealed that he'd held up a convenience store when he was 18.

"Just a really idiotic impulse. Christ knows what I was thinking," he said, shaking his head.

He'd hit the clerk over the head when the guy tried to grab him over the counter. Turns out the man ended up with a concussion and couldn't remember a thing about the robbery. That was back before they had video cameras all over the place.

Thus Frank got away with it and vowed never to break the law again. The whole experience really shook him up. It was hard for us to believe he actually did such a thing, because he was one of the straightest people around. A retired school principal and good all around citizen. Even taught Bible school, for heaven's sake. He said he felt so bad for the guy he injured that when he got a few dollars saved up, he sent it to him anonymously. Imagine that. Now that's someone with a conscience.

The next member of our group that surprised us with what he confessed was Gabe Copeland.

"I think I raped a girl back in college," he said, his eyes averted from ours.

"What do you mean you *think* you raped someone?" I asked.

"Well, we were both pretty drunk. She was in my dorm room and my roommate was out. We got kissing and then I unbuttoned the back of her blouse. She didn't try to stop me. Pretty soon I had her bra and skirt off and was on top of her. When I tried to put it in, she said 'don't,' but I kept going. She told me to stop, but I didn't. When I was done, she just lay there kind of whimpering. I said I was sorry, but she put her clothes back on and left. We never talked after that, but whenever I saw her, she'd give me this look like I was some kind of monster."

"Hey, you two were drunk. Don't beat yourself up over it, Gabe. You were just kids, too. We all do dumb things when we're young and horned out of our minds," said Sam Connors.

"Yeah, but when I think of what I did, I think of my youngest daughter when she was assaulted at college. She didn't get raped but damn near did. If it wasn't for someone hearing her scream, she would have."

"Wow, didn't know that Gabe, but that was a different situation. You didn't attack that girl. You guys were friends and tying one on together. What did she expect? She knew where you were going when you took her clothes off."

"I don't know, Sam. It's kind of like splitting hairs. She told me to stop, and I didn't," said Gabe, his voice trailing off.

The following week brought another jarring revelation, this one from Sam himself.

"I double billed my clients to avoid paying so much in taxes. Saved a fortune, and the IRS never caught up to me. That was two decades ago. Finally came to my senses and stopped. But if it wasn't for that I never would have been able to buy all the things we have or go on so many cruises with Millie."

"Well, shit, who doesn't cheat on their taxes?" said Frank.

"Yeah, but not to the tune of a half million dollars," replied Sam.

"You're lucky you weren't caught. The feds would have locked you up forever," I said.

"Is there a statute of limitation on tax fraud? Like I said, it was a long time ago. Hope none of you guys tell anybody about this," remarked Sam, now looking slightly anxious.

"Yeah, what do you say, guys? Should we blow the whistle on this income tax evader?" I joked.

"Why not?" said Gabe. "And while we're at it we can report Frank's robbery and my rape. A win-win all around."

"Well, I may as well throw my hat into this ring of fire. And I use that term literally," said Mel Kagan.

Mel was typically the least talkative of our group, but when he had something to say, it was usually worth listening to.

"You remember the fire that gutted my store seven years ago? That wasn't caused by faulty wiring, like they reported."

"Oh, shit," we mumbled, knowing what was coming.

"Yup, I torched the place. I owed thousands to my suppliers and business was plain rotten. I didn't want to declare bankruptcy, so I did the nasty. Collected on the insurance, and decided not to rebuild. For a long time I thought they'd reinvestigate the fire, but they never did. I guess like the rest of you guys, I dodged the bullet."

"Hey, all's well that ends well, right?" said Sam, and we all agreed.

"So this is a real den of thieves. Who would have thought?" commented Frank.

The next time we got together, I was put in the box.

"Hey, Denny, time to air your dirty laundry. What's the big, dark secret in your life? Time to fess up, old pal" said Sam.

"Well, I'm far from perfect . . . that's for sure. But I haven't committed any *real* crimes. Done some stupid things . . . yes to that one. We all have, but not a felony. Got speeding tickets more than once."

"C'mon, Denny . . . speeding tickets? That's it?" said Frank, exasperated.

"Don't hold back. We all leveled about our past indiscretions," added Gabe.

"Sorry, guys. I just never did anything as . . ."

"*Bad* as we did, you mean?" scowled Sam.

"No, I didn't mean that. Guess I just haven't led as colorful a life as you guys."

"Well, you got the goods on us now, don't you?" said Frank, his brow furrowing.

After a long, awkward silence, the group dispersed for the day. When I showed up at the garage the next morning, there was a note taped on the back door:

"Non-felons unwelcome."

I was so angry I gave the door a hard kick. As I walked away, I heard laughter rise up behind me. When I turned around, Frank, Gabe, Sam, and Mel greeted me, their widespread arms beckoning.

"Where the hell do you think you're going, Mr. Goody Two-Shoes?" asked Gabe, and then I was locked in an affectionate embrace by my once miscreant chums.

However, despite this reassuring gesture, things were never quite the same between the guys and me. Eventually, I stopped showing up at the garage because I felt like an outsider. The whole thing made me wish I had committed a crime at some point in my past.

#

Existential

She snores.
 I fart.
There you have it.
 Yeah . . . there you have it.

#

Signings

*Authors have always faced a tough path: chronic rejection, no
job security, and low pay . . . if you're lucky.*

—Ron Charles

Shad Newburg was excited that his publisher was arranging a
regional book signing for his first novel—a thriller—even
though they had originally said he'd be reading all across the
country. The abbreviated tour would take him to several
towns and cities around New England. He would drive
himself to the events, since he lived in Worcester,
Massachusetts, which was centrally located to where most of
the signings were to take place. All of his friends and
members of his family were impressed with the forthcoming
excursions and were certain they would be a great success.
Shad hoped they were right and was keen to get started.

A week after *Dark Nights* published he was scheduled to read
in Manchester, Connecticut. The bookstore was on the main
street and wedged between two empty storefronts. Two
people sat in the row of folding chairs as Shad took the
podium. Since it was his first ever reading, he was nervous
and somewhat relieved that there were so few attendees.

"Thank you, ladies and gentlemen . . . er, I mean *ladies*," said
Shad, noticing that no males were present. I appreciate your
coming, and I want to thank the *Furry Pen* for having me."

Just as Shad was about to launch into his reading, one of the
women suddenly stood up and walked away, looking as if she
just remembered that she had to be somewhere else. Shad
was distracted by her abrupt departure and sputtered the first
few words of the chapter he intended to read. *Please don't leave*,
he pleaded to himself, fearing the last remaining member of
the audience might also make for an exit.

When he had finished his reading 20 minutes later, the sole attendee applauded vigorously and got up and quickly vanished. Only a couple of people remained in the bookstore as Shad sat behind the table that held a small stack of his books. A hand written sign invited patrons to "meet the author."

"You really don't have to hang around," said the bookstore manager. "It looks like a real slow day here. Sorry, but I suspect you'd be wasting your time. Thanks for coming though. Too bad there wasn't a better turnout."

Shad returned home and when his friends and family asked how it went, he told them that attendance was good as were sales of his book. He was too embarrassed and disappointed to tell the truth, and the last thing he wanted was any sympathy. He'd received so much attention for getting his book published that he didn't want people to think it was all for naught.

Just a fluke, he told himself about the less than stellar experience in Manchester. *Providence will be better. It's a bigger city, and the bookstore is much larger.* Three days later he drove to that engagement feeling renewed optimism. He arrived at the store early and wandered the aisles before officially reporting in. All the while, he kept his eyes on the section of the store obviously set up for author readings.

As the time for his reading approached, several people took their seats and Shad felt an electric charge stream through his body. *Okay, now this is what I mean*, he mumbled happily. His joy was quickly shattered when he revealed his identity to a bookstore staffer.

"Oh, *Mary Hartwell* is reading from her book today. There must have been some kind of mix-up. Let me get Jean."

When the store manager confirmed that, indeed, he was not scheduled to read from his book, Shad's heart sunk.

"We had to adjust the line up because Hartwell could only be here today. You were rescheduled for next Wednesday. You should have received a notice about this. It was emailed to you yesterday. I realize it was short notice, but we didn't want to miss out on Mary Hartwell, because her book has just entered the bestseller list. We were certain you'd get the notice about the change. Really sorry that you didn't."

Shad was upset, but he concealed his displeasure and resisted challenging the bookstore manager about the email, although he was certain he had not received it.

"Look why don't you stay for the reading and the wine reception that follows," offered the manager of *The Thumbed Page*, but Shad was too disheartened to stick around.

On his return trip home, he tried to buoy his slumping spirits before he faced his family. *Schedules get screwed up all the time. No biggie . . . right? It wasn't cancelled, and the crowd was huge. Could be huge for mine, too,'* Shad told himself, but his gloom's heavy grip could not be loosened. *She's a bestselling author, you idiot. That's why all those people were there. You'll be lucky if three people show up for yours.*

Shad was almost right. Again, just two people sat before him as he read from his debut novel. He was thankful that both remained seated until he finished but felt disheartened when only one individual purchased a copy of *Dark Nights*. He remained at the small author's table for the better part of two hours. During that time, the scant number of customers in the store paid him little attention.

"Glad you were able to come back," said the store manager. "Again, I'm sorry about the schedule mix up. By the way, I really like the cover of your book. Too bad you didn't have more people at your reading. Been a slow day for some reason. You never know when people will show up, although, Hartwell drew a lot of people last week. She was really wonderful."

"Right," said Shad, as he collected himself to leave. "Her book is on the bestseller list. This is only my first novel."

"It takes time before readers know who you are. All writers start out this way. I've even had a couple better know authors here that only attracted a couple of people like you did. Don't get discouraged."

Shad took solace in the bookstore manager's words, and clung to them on his drive home. Once again, he painted a positive picture of his reading, telling everyone that it was fun . . . and profitable as well.

"I bet you'll end up on Oprah," said his best friend, and Shad snickered. "Well, why not? People like your book, and it's really good. Who knows?"

"It's not that easy, Clark. You have to sell a million copies before that happens."

"Well, you're on your way."

"Yeah, sold *one* lousy . . . *er*, I mean a *few dozen* copies. Long way from a million."

"*Dark Nights* will be a bestseller. It just came out a couple weeks ago, right? You wait and see. I know it will."

"Thanks for your encouragement, man. But I'm not holding my breath."

"Don't do that. Doctors say it's not good for you," chuckled Clark. "Hey, are you writing another?"

"Yeah, I mentioned I was writing something new a few months back."

"Did you? Well, you've kept it kind of quiet. Cool."

"Just have to get it to my publisher. They have first turn down."

"What . . .?"

"My contract says they get to look at my next novel before I send it any place else."

"Oh, they'll dig it. You said they loved *Dark Nights.*"

"We'll see. I do think the new one is good."

"Hell, yes, it's *good.* You da man. Don't forget your old buddy when you're famous."

* * *

Springfield, Massachusetts, was the next stop on Shad's reading schedule, and it was there he had his largest turn out. All of six people were sitting in the metal folding chairs scattered willy-nilly about the rear of the bookstore. As he took his place at the lectern after a brief introduction by a store employee, he noticed that two members of the audience were fiddling with their smart phones while another was paging through a copy of *Vanity Fair.*

Overall, Shad was pleased with his reading and was about to move to the signing table when the person who'd been reading the magazine raised her hand and posed a question.

"Are you going to write a sequel?"

"I already have," answered Shad, pleased with the inquiry.

"You should. People like sequels."

"Thank you," replied Shad, waiting for other questions until it was obvious there would be none.

When he headed to the signing table, no one followed, and only a few shoppers glanced his way during the next hour.

Guess it's been another slow day? he mumbled cynically, as the bookstore staffer came up to him.

"If you want to sign a couple copies of your book, we'll keep them in the store, but we'll have to send the rest back to your publisher."

After responding to the staffer's request, Shad returned home reporting that all had gone well at *The Last Chapter*. He was tempted to reveal the truth to his mother, but her never waning enthusiasm for whatever he accomplished discouraged his doing so. His next reading was at *The Word Wabbit* in Keene, New Hampshire. By now, Shad had little hope that it would be anything but another disappointment. However, he continued to hold out hope that things would take a turn for the better.

On the day he was to set out for New Hampshire, *The Worcester Free Paper* ran a short but positive review of his book. It lifted his mood considerably and made the 70-mile drive northwest far more enjoyable than it would have been. Unfortunately, the low turnout for his reading, and the subsequent lack of sales, made the trip home a dreary one. *Why should I even do these things? A waste of time and freaking embarrassing. Don't bother any more, Shad,* he told himself but knew he'd fulfill the last of the dates his publisher had scheduled.

His next signing was in Maine at *The Howling Shelf*—over five hours away. It was set for 1 PM on Sunday, so he planned to leave his house around 7 AM, which would give him time to grab some lunch before arriving. It had occurred to Shad to get a hotel room for the night rather than drive all the way home after his appearance, but he was running low on money and was reluctant to ask his publisher to pick up the tab, since they had already indicated a lack of funds for his travels. "We can cover your mileage, but that's about it," they had said at the outset.

Due to roadwork, Shad arrived at the bookstore just minutes before the reading was scheduled to start. He was immediately greeted by a chirpy, middle-age woman, who reminded him of his fourth grade teacher, Mrs. Hodges. Shad had always thought very kindly of her, because she treated him with exceptional patience and understanding as he dealt with his slight stutter. Despite the fact that he'd worked with a speech therapist for two years, he attributed his overcoming the mild but embarrassing impediment directly to the extra time she'd devoted to him.

"Well, hello. Mr. Newburg. Welcome to *The Howling Shelf*. It's so good to have you here. I'm Dolly Cummings, the proprietor. Your audience awaits you, as you can see. Why don't we get right to it, okay?"

After a very warm introduction by Cummings, Shad thanked the audience—he counted eight attendees in all—for coming and then launched into his reading, giving it all the enthusiasm he could muster. As he started reading, he noticed someone sitting behind a display table with a pyramid of travel books. All he could see were legs and hands, and he wondered why anyone would bother coming to an author's event and then hide himself during it.

To his disappointment, no questions were asked when his reading was over, but the round of applause that followed it pleased him.

"Thank you very much. If anyone would like to purchase a book, I'd be happy to sign it."

Shad sat at the author's table and waited for customers. Only one person came up to him, and in a near whisper she asked if he was related to the Sam Newburgh who owned the town's hardware store. When he politely told her he was not, she shrugged her shoulders and walked away. *Here we go again. No buyers . . . never any buyers. That's it. This is my last signing, not that I've been signing anything. Ridiculous,* Shad grumbled to himself.

Just as he was about to gather himself together for his long drive back home, the person who had been sitting behind the book display toward the back of the event area, emerged and moved toward him. *A buyer . . . could be,* he thought, mildly optimistically.

"I liked what you read. Some nice writing there. Keep at it," said the lean, bearded man, who then shook Shad's hand and slipped from the bookstore.

Okay, if you liked it so much, why didn't you buy a copy? thought Shad, more than mildly exasperated.

"Mr. Newburgh!" said Dolly Cummings, approaching him excitedly. "Do you know who that was?"

"No, but he didn't buy a book," replied Shad, attempting to put a lighthearted spin on his words but failing dismally.

"That was Stephen King. I saw him speaking with you."

"*Stephen King*? No kidding, really?" Jeez, he did look familiar . . . *The* Stephen King? You sure?"

"Absolutely. He lives here in Bangor and comes in from time to time. But I never saw him speak with a guest author before. What did he tell you?"

After a thoughtful pause, Shad answered. "Exactly what I needed to hear."

#

Reader

After Cary read Ray Bradbury's *Dandelion Wine*, he wanted to hold the writer's head between his hands and kiss it to be as close to his mind as possible. He believed that it was there that all the power and beauty of humanity existed.

#

Tot Finder

Now I know what a ghost is. Unfinished business, that's what a ghost is.

—Salman Rushdie

Back in the 1970s, local fire departments distributed home window stickers designed to alert firefighters as to the whereabouts of young children in the event of a conflagration. Over time, the youngsters in residence grew up and moved on. While the stickers faded, many remained where they'd first been placed.

Josh Willoughby had affixed a decal to his three year-old daughter's bedroom window and had slept easier because of it. He had been in a near tragic fire as a child in the three-decker apartment he occupied with his parent's in the 1950's. He had lived with the dread of experiencing such a horrific incident again.

As he stuck the Tot Finder alert to his daughter Willow's window, he explained its purpose in language he hoped she could understand.

"Remember when you saw *Smokey the Bear* on television say, 'Only you can prevent forest fires?' Well, sometimes houses also catch fire. If that ever happens, the fireman will carry you to safety just like he is the little girl in this picture, okay, honey?"

"Okay, Daddy. He's a *nice* man."

"Yes, he is, sweetheart. Yes, he *is*," said Josh, attempting to imitate Smokey's basso profondo.

In the weeks that followed, Willow became fixated on the sticker, parading around the house gleefully chanting, "The fireman saved me," over and over.

The horrible irony that his daughter died *not* from fire but from water defined the dark days to come. Barely five, Willow would be found floating unconscious in a neighbor's above ground pool. This tragedy marked the end of the happiest period in Josh's life. He had married his high school sweetheart and begun his career as an electrician when the scaffolding was pulled out from under him.

Within a year, he had lost everything he cherished. The strain of their daughter's death was too much for the marriage to withstand, because he blamed his wife for not watching their child when she was visiting a friend. And the heavy drinking he took up to drown his sorrows soon cost him his job. Only several years later did Josh regain his footing on what had been a bumpy and ragged path.

Although, he'd been convinced that his existence would never again contain joy, he met and fell in love with a woman he'd met at an AA meeting. She was not an alcoholic, but had accompanied her brother to the meeting. There they caught one another's eye. At first, he felt some guilt over finding some much-needed happiness, but over time he came to realize that life need not be just unrelenting gloom.

As the years passed, Josh eventually found success as the owner of a small electrical service company. His second wife had not pressed the issue of having kids and that was fine with him. He could not fathom the idea of bringing another child into the world after the heartbreak he'd gone through.

Yet despite his happier days, Josh never forgot about his lost daughter, and his sense of pain became especially acute around the anniversary of her death. Now, as the day approached again, Josh found himself feeling particularly low. *Forty*, he reminded himself. *She would have been forty years old next week. How could that be? Impossible. My little baby . . .*

Although, Josh generally avoided passing the house where he'd lived when Willow was alive, he suddenly felt an urged to see it on this particular anniversary of his daughter's deadly accident. The home was located in a nearby town and, in fact, he'd passed the end of his old street many times over the years. But he'd always kept from looking in the direction of the house, fearing the pain it might cause him.

Turning onto his old street, he caught sight of the house where Willow had spent her short life. It had been repainted and its sagging decks were rebuilt. He pulled up across from it and looked at the second floor flat. Then he noticed the Tot Finder sticker he had placed on his daughter's window. It was faded so that the image of the fireman and child he held were barely discernable. Seeing it brought back the memory of kneeling at the window next to his daughter and telling her about the significance of the sticker. The bittersweet recollection was quickly followed by the hysterical voice of his wife telling him of their child's drowning.

Josh closed his eyes and clutched the steering wheel. *Willow . . . Willow. I'm so sorry, honey. Your life was so short. I miss you so much.* With tears rolling down his cheeks, he looked again at the window of his daughter's former bedroom. *What?* he gulped, as he saw the figure of a young child. *Willow . . . no, it can't be. Are you really . . .?* He cleared the tears from his eyes, and looked again. The gossamer image of the small girl remained. "Oh, Willow," he whimpered, waving up at the window.

In the next moment, the child was gone, and Josh climbed from his car and went to the house. Shortly after ringing the bell to the second floor apartment, a young woman appeared.

"I'm sorry to bother you, but I used to live here, and I noticed that the Tot Finder sticker I put on my daughter's bedroom window 40 years ago is still there."

"Oh, really? That's right, it is. We were going to remove it but forgot about it. We don't use the room. Only store things in it."

"But, I thought . . . well, for a moment, I thought I saw a little girl looking out of the window. She actually looked like my daughter."

"We don't have any kids. Maybe it was just a reflection of the kids next door. They often play in the yard."

"Maybe . . . could be," said Josh, feeling embarrassed. "I'm probably seeing things. It's the anniversary of my daughter's accident. She drowned in a pool a few houses down from here."

"I'm so sorry," said the woman. After an awkward pause, she continued. "If you like, we'll keep the sticker on the window."

Josh gulped hard to keep from letting out a sob. "That would be so kind. It's very special to me. It's kind of like finding her again. I mean . . ."

"Of course, we won't touch it."

After exchanging goodbyes, Josh returned to his car. Before he drove away, he looked back up at his daughter's window. And again, he made out the vision of a small child's face pressed against the glass next the Tot Finder sticker. But this time he also heard her sweet voice:

The fireman saved me. The fireman saved me.

Josh closed his eyes and listened intently until the sound of his daughter's precious words had faded completely.

"Yes . . . yes, he *did*, sweetheart," he whispered.

#

Oops!!

Margery was passive aggressive, or so her husband kept telling her.

"And how do you know that? What makes you the expert?" she asked.

"Because you keep the things that really bother you all pent up and attack the little things to vent your built up anger.

"Like what, Dr. Freud? Please tell me."

"Okay, the other day you got all over my case because I tracked a little dirt onto the livingroom rug. You yelled like a crazed banshee. You'd have thought I set fire to the house."

"So what should I have been taking my *true* anger out on? Give me one good example, Mr. Know-It-All."

"Yeah, well you haven't brought up anything about the panties you found in the back seat of my . . . *I mean,* " stammered Ben, dropping his glass of tomato juice.

"Asshole! You spilled your drink on the *new* placemats," shrieked Margery, reaching for a carving knife.

#

Directions to America

They've all come to look for America.
— Paul Simon

After considering how to get me across town to where I was to meet up with a colleague, the hotel doorman decided it was easier just to use prominent city landmarks along the way instead of street names. I was determined to walk rather than take a taxi. I needed the exercise, I explained, having spent two days on a plane from New Zealand.

"Your call, buddy" he shrugged "So better write this down, okay?"

I removed a notebook and pen from my coat and signaled that I was ready. He lifted his gloved hand and pointed.

"You head down this street to the Taco Bell and take a left two blocks until you reach the McDonalds. Take a right when you get there and go four blocks to the Wendy's. You're going to take another right for a block and turn left at the Duncan Donuts. You might want to grab a hot one because you'll be shivering your timbers by then in this freaking cold. Got it so far?"

"Yes," I replied.

"After DDs, go about three, maybe four, blocks up 8th Street to the Pizza Hut. You'll be about halfway to your friend's by then.

A sudden icy gust pushed both of us against the revolving door that led into the Hilton's lobby.

"Sure you don't want a cab? It's kind of a bitch out here."

I declined his offer again, and he gave me a skeptical look before continuing with his instructions.

"Okay then, so now you're going to hoof it left two blocks to the Subway and hang a right for another three blocks when you get to the Arby's. From there, just go straight until you reach the Burger King. Take your right there, and you'll see the United Nations building. You got that? Read it back to me."

"Sure, okay. So I go down to Taco Bell. Left two blocks to McDonalds. Right four blocks to Wendy's. Right again to Duncan Donuts. Turn left three or four blocks to the Pizza Hut. Take another left two blocks to the Subway and turn right three blocks to the Arby's. Go straight from there to the Burger King. Take a right and I'll be able to see the U.N. Sound right?"

"Yeah, I guess you got it all. Hey, it'll only take you 10 minutes by cab and you won't freeze your buns off. What do you say, pal? Don't want you to get frost bite on your visit to our country."

"No thanks," I said. "I wouldn't want to miss seeing first-hand some of America's most iconic landmarks."

#

Clean Underpants

Hundreds of people look up to me, but where are my clean underpants?

My company provides their livelihoods, but where are my clean underpants?

Without me they'd be without shelter, but where are my clean underpants?

Everyone treats me with such respect, but where are my clean underpants?

The media praise my business acumen, but where are my clean underpants?

My achievements are legendary, but where are my clean underpants?

Dozens of awards adorn my office walls, but where are my clean underpants?

I've had such an enviable career, but where are my clean underpants?

At some point, I'll run for high office, but where are my clean underpants?

The nation would benefit from my great knowledge and wisdom . . .

But damn! *Where* the hell are my clean underpants?

#

Mascot

If you pick up a starving dog and make him
prosperous he will not bite you. This is the principal
difference between a dog and a man.
                    —Mark Twain

Something moved in the grass ahead as I walked toward the line of portable toilets that were kept at a sanitary distance from the base's housing and administrative buildings. *Snake!!* *Everglades is full of them, even at its fringes,* warned the voice in my head, and I froze in my tracks. *Maybe a rattler or coral,* I speculated, swinging long to my right to give the possible viper wide berth. There was another slight movement, and I stepped away even further.

But then I could see that whatever the creature was, it had fur. *Could be a skunk or rabbit.* It then lifted its head and made a sorrowful sound. *A dog . . . it's a dog. Or what is left of one. Careful, it's probably rabid. Don't let it nip you. Needle in the belly,* I told myself, slowly approaching the distressed animal.

A badly emaciated hound stared up at me with its milky eyes and then shut them as if it took all the remaining energy it had to open them.

"Hey, fella'. You still alive?" I asked, thinking it may have just died.

On closer inspection, I could detect faint breathing. "You're a skeleton. You need some food and water right away. I'll be right back."

I sprinted to the mess tent and grabbed several pieces of bread that remained piled next to the breakfast toasters. From there, I fetched my canteen from my tent and filled it with water. Within minutes I was back at the site of the dying, or now dead, animal. As soon as I took the bread from my fatigue jacket, it raised its wobbly head.

"Still alive, eh? Good. Here you go," I said, dropping a slice next to its snout.

A split second after the bread hit the ground, it disappeared into the starving hound's maw.

"Whoa, fella'. There's more where that came from. Here we are."

Again, the dog gulped down the bread, hardly bothering to chew it.

"Water? Here's some water," I said, opening the canteen and pouring some of its contents into the dog's mouth. As it drank, it whimpered softly. "Yeah, that's what you want, eh, fella'? I'll get a bowl the next time."

My canteen was quickly emptied, but the dog's thirst had clearly not been fully satisfied. "Okay, I'll go get some more, pooch" I promised, giving it the last piece of bread I had.

When it was through licking its chops with its discolored and swollen tongue, its head fell limply against the burnt grass. Its bony chest cavity moved rapidly as if eating and drinking had been a great physical challenge.

"What happened to you? How'd you get in such bad shape?"

For a moment, I was tempted to pet what remained of its fur, but it's mangy appearance kept me from doing so. The surface of its depleted body looked as if it had met with a ragged blade. Small sores zigzagged across its exposed flanks.

"Never saw anything in such rough shape. Poor thing," I said, touching its scrawny tail.

This caused it to growl and move slightly. "That's okay. I'm going to help you. See you soon."

I returned near sunset and fed it several hot dogs—tube steaks, as GIs called 'em—that I'd managed to collect from disposed supper trays.

"You into eating garbage now, Cary?" asked the mess sergeant, as I wrapped the throwaways in a napkin.

"Found a starving dog in the field and thought I'd help it out," I responded.

"Well, take all you want. Better than throwing it out, I suppose."

"It'll probably die anyway. Think it's a Collie, but it's hard to tell because it's so wasted away. Its fur has pretty much fallen off."

"Thing don't sound too pretty. If it makes it to tomorrow, I'll have some steak bones to give you."

"Thanks, Sarg. I appreciate it. Hope it makes it until then, too."

After the still famished dog had devoured the leftovers, I gave it a carton of milk in a bowl I'd borrowed from the mess tent. For the first time, the mutt managed to raise its haunches enough to guzzle the liquid.

"Good boy. You're getting stronger. Maybe you'll get your legs back soon."

When the bowl was empty, the dog looked at me appreciatively and flopped back on its side. As it did so, I bent down and pat its head. At first it pulled away but then submitted to my touch.

"Thataboy. We're friends now, right? I'll be back in the morning," I said, surveying the ground around us. "Looks safe, fella. No snakes to hurt you. Sleep and get back your strength."

* * *

When I told my tent mates about my discovery, they were less than sympathetic about its dire situation.

"Should probably just put it out of its misery. Sounds about done in anyway. It's probably full of crud, like worms and stuff that'll eat it alive. Careful you don't catch something from it," said Wayne.

"Yeah, not worth the effort. Even if it gets better, so what? Just another varmint scavenging out here. End up dying anyway the shape it's in," added Jerry.

"What about Scooter and Blackie? They were strays and now they're fine. All you guys love them," I argued.

Scooter and Blackie had become the base's official mascots since their arrival a year ago. One day, the two mongrels just showed up and they were quickly adopted. Of course, they weren't nearly as bad off as the one in the field, so they grossed no one out. Only a couple guys from the motor pool had wanted to throw them into the snake-infested canal.

"If that thing gets close to the tent area, Scooter will probably do it in. He's got a lot of Shepherd in him, and they're really protective of what's theirs," continued Jerry.

"And if it gets near Blackie, Scooter will chomp its head off. Jealous of his lady," said Wayne.

"Maybe not," I protested. "Dogs can make friends. That poor fella' out there is no threat. Scooter will sense that."

"Well, that bag of bones better not come 'round here. He'll infest Scooter and Blackie with what he's got . . . maybe Rabies. Better not let it bite you," warned Jerry.

"It frothing at the mouth?" asked Wayne. "Maybe we should go check it out."

"Leave it alone. Just a sad stray whose had it tough," I objected. "Don't go making things worse for it."

* * *

Over the next few days, my canine patient improved as I continued to feed it everything I could get from the mess tent. There was nothing it wouldn't eat. About a week after I'd come upon the pitiful critter, it was able to stand and take a few tentative steps.

Meanwhile, my fellow soldiers kept saying it should be put out of its misery before it came into contact with Scooter and Blackie.

"I'm surprised they haven't sniffed out its rotting carcass by now. Probably have and won't go near it," said Wayne

"I saw it on the way to the head last night, and it was dragging its rump. Bet it's got an ass full of maggots. Crap them around Scooter and Blackie, and they'll get 'em, too," said Jerry.

"One good whack in the head and no more *problemo*," added Wayne, raising his fist and swinging it for emphasis.

"Just let him be. He's not harming anything and is getting better every day," I said, heading out of the tent to continue my doctoring.

The next morning brought a shock when I woke up and found the stray curled up at the foot of Wayne's bunk . . . with Wayne asleep in it.

Jesus, he'll kill him if he sees that. How'd he get there? I wondered, my pulse quickening as I slipped over to where the ragged dog snoozed seemingly unaware of any danger. I gently lifted it from the bed, and as I did, Wayne spoke.

"Where you taken 'Rattle?" he asked, rubbing the sleep from his eyes.

"Look, I don't know how he got in and up on your bunk," I sputtered, anticipating an explosion.

"I do," said Wayne, stroking the dog's back. "I put him there. That a problem?"

"Why would you . . .? I mean, I thought you wanted to get rid of him."

"That was my plan last night when I went out to bust its head. But as I was about to club him, he ran behind me. Next thing I know he's got a rattler by the neck and is shakin' the hell out of it. Old boy got to the friggin' snake before it sunk its fangs into me. Saved my hide . . . right, Rattle? Hey, know why I named him Rattle?"

"I can guess," I answered.

Wayne climbed from his bunk and put on his pants as I stood trying to digest everything he'd just told me.

"C'mon, Rattle, time for us to get some breakfast," said Wayne, walking out of the tent with his new friend at his side.

While I was thankful that the stray had found a new and unlikely guardian, I felt a bit abandoned by the creature I'd saved from a certain death. It took me a while to overcome my sense of betrayal and more fully appreciate the fact that my former patient was alive and well. In the end, that's what was most important, and I could take solace in my part in that.

During the balance of my time in the military in South Florida, Rattle achieved the status of top dog at the small missile base that had been erected during the Cuban Missile Crisis. He quickly made friends with Scooter and Blackie, and it soon became obvious to everyone that they regarded him as their leader. Rattle showed a level of maturity and gentleness that gained him the respect of the camp's soldiers as well.

The day I was discharged, I gave Rattle a long goodbye hug. By now, most of his fur had returned. Before I had finished my farewell, he dashed off in the direction of Wayne, who was approaching from a distance away.

"Take good care of him," I shouted.

"You don't have to worry about that," Wayne answered, his arms spread wide to greet his best friend . . . and savior.

#

It Was a Book That Revised Itself

Published in 1946, the novel had updated its contents to reflect the realities of life in 2015.

As Harris read the old mystery, it struck him that something was not right. The sentence that caught his eye read as follows:

Matilda placed the smoking Glock into her backpack and removed her cellphone to call Randy at Starbucks.

"*What!* Oh, c'mon! This is crazy. Dumb book," he grumbled. "Glocks *don't* smoke after you fire them."

Harris knew this for a fact, because he was an arms expert . . . if not the most intuitive reader.

#

The Duke Beats Up the Bad Guys

Kids can be very shrewd.
—Maurice Sendak

My father was working the day shift, so as usual I tried to find something to do to get me out of our one room efficiency apartment, as he called it. If I was lucky the movie had changed at the Redland, the only place they even had movies in the small town we were stuck in. I say stuck in because that's where our trip to California had stalled and where my father took a job running the elevator at the Calmez Hotel.

We'd been in town for three weeks and I was more than a little anxious to get going again. Oklahoma was only halfway to our destination from Richmond, where we had started and where I was born. My parents were divorced, and it was my time with my father, because that's the way it worked out in the summers when school was out. This time we decided to go on a long trip west instead of making our usual local ones a few hundred miles up or down the East Coast.

The only problem with our plan was we lacked the money for a bus ticket all the way out west. But my father figured it wouldn't be tough hitching a ride from where what money he had for a ticket would take us. He was wrong. After our ride on the Greyhound out to Memphis, it took us a week to get to Clinton, Oklahoma.

Now our plan was to buy another ticket, hopefully as far as Albuquerque, when he got his check. He'd saved a few dollars from his previous checks and with his next one we could afford to get underway again. His theory held that we could catch some long distant rides from Albuquerque, because there wasn't that many towns for people to be going to between it and California.

I dreamed of our departure date set for the following Monday as I checked out the matinee. To my delight it had changed from the boring Sandra Dee movie that had been playing over the last week. John Wayne was starring in something called *Rio Bravo*, and I was excited to see it as I handed over my quarter to the lady in the ticket booth. That's all it cost for kids up to 12, and I was just barely under that age limit. The movie was halfway over when I entered the dark theater. But that was fine, because I would sit through it until it returned to the part where I came in. I took a seat about midway down toward the front and nestled in as the Duke was punching out some mean looking gunslingers.

Not long after I became engrossed in the action on the screen, I heard someone whispering. I looked at the rows ahead and noticed a lone figure waving in my direction. I looked around and saw no one sitting behind me that might be the target of his wave. At first I pretended not to notice, but when the man continued flapping his hand toward me, I leaned forward in my seat and in a low voice asked what he wanted.

"Why don't you come up here with me? We're the only ones in the place. More fun to watch a movie with someone else," he said.

"Okay," I replied, thinking he was trying to be friendly, and I longed for companionship, since I had made no friends in the time we'd been in Clinton.

"You like this movie?" he asked as I slipped into the seat next to him.

"Yeah, I love westerns," I answered.

"You want a Jujy Fruits. Here have some."

"Thanks, I replied, more than willing to share his candy, as I hadn't had money to buy my own.

We sat in silence for a while gazing intently at the screen and then he asked if I would do him a favor.

"Sure," I answered.

"Touch me."

"What?" I asked, startled and not knowing what he meant.

"Here . . . put your hand on me and rub."

The stranger took my hand and moved it onto something I immediately realized was his private. Although, I tried to pull my hand away, he held it in place. Suddenly I was overcome by fear, thinking he would get mad if I didn't do what he said. My head swirled as I tried to figure out what to do. As the movie drew to its climax, an idea struck me.

"I better go. My dad is a policeman, and he said he'd meet me in the lobby after the movie," I said, trying to appear calm.

"Your father's a cop?" he replied, pushing my hand away from his lap. "No, you're kidding."

"Yeah, he's a sergeant in the force. Would you like to meet him?" I offered, continuing my charade.

"Look, I got to go, kid. See you sometime. Don't say nothing to . . ." said the man, tugging at his fly.

He rose abruptly and scampered up the isle without saying anything further. I remained in my seat for the movie to start up again thinking proudly about how I had managed to get myself out of a really weird situation. I decided it wasn't anything I'd tell my father.

#

Half Lives

— Mary and Harold go to Disney World every year.

— Susan has 6 kids and is planning on having another.

— Kyle considers the Venetian in Las Vegas better than Venice itself.

— The Johnsons only go for a drive on Sundays.

— Sarah raves about the clothes and shoes at Wal-Mart.

— "The Bold and the Beautiful" is high drama to Jill.

— Marvin and Kelli fight over which buffet restaurant is best.

— Craig is driven crazy when dandelions appear in his yard.

— Floyd Lipchitz buys a white Toyota Corolla.

— Peggy Taylor watches *The Sound of Music* 37 times.

— Chicken McNuggets are Dale's favorite food.

— Basil Rumford considers watching his lawn sprinkler an activity.

— The Williams think humans are not meant to fly so take the bus cross-country.

— Gladys moves to Sun City instead of Tahiti with her boyfriend.

— Sam gets a canary for company.

— A fun-filled, getaway weekend for the Taylors means a stay at Motel 6.

— Helen always drives 5 MPH under the speed limit.

— Percy's favorite dessert is Fig Newton.

— The Wilsons believe America is always right.

#

Is a Funeral Home *Really* a Home?

*You can't stop being afraid just by pretending
everything that scares you isn't there.*
                              —Michael Marshall

During the summer of my 11th year, I lived with the dead. It was a period during which I came to know the real limits of my fear. In my child's overactive imagination, there were corpses watching me from every dark corner of the funeral home where we were temporarily living. This was especially true at night, when I was left alone in the top floor bedroom I shared with my father. In my young mind, these were the hours when the most recently deposited cadaver lifted itself from the metal embalming table two floors below and came in hungry pursuit of . . . me. I had seen plenty of zombie movies, and I expected to have the flesh torn off my bones at any moment as I burrowed under the bedcovers for safety—sweating from every pore.

My father's first cousin, Doris Roebacker, operated the stately looking mortuary in East Hartford, Connecticut, and she offered us the chance to stay in its well-appointed resident quarters. She knew my father was trying to get himself back together after a bout with the bottle, although he didn't admit that to her—in point of fact, his alcoholism was something he wouldn't admit to himself.

At first, I was thrilled to be occupying a building that looked so classy and respectable, but then it quickly sunk in that this ornate place was where the dead were prepped for the afterlife. Almost immediately I began to wish we were be back on the road or in some homeless shelter—even a roach infested rented room. I figured anything would be better than sharing a roof with dead people.

Yet again, I cursed my father for his irresponsible behavior. In my view, it was his excessive drinking that screwed up everything, putting us in many unpleasant situations. But I had chosen to go with him rather than remain behind in a more stable—and certainly less exciting—environment with my mother and sisters. So I tried to accept the consequences of my decision, although it sure was not easy at times. And this was surely one of *those* times. *If I were back with Mom, I wouldn't be about to be attacked by the undead,* I brooded, my anger growing as the bed sheets became saturated with my sweat.

* * *

On the other hand, staying at the funeral home did have its lighter moments. My father's cousin was a very cheery person, despite her dreary occupation. When Aunt Doris, as she told me to call her, was not at work on her clients, she was in her kitchen humming tunes and sharing jokes with my father. *How can she be so happy when she works with dead people?* I wondered, but I was glad she wasn't like the undertakers I'd seen in horror movies. They always looked as grim and pale as the bodies they experimented with or attempted to revive.

Early on in what would be a short stay, I had found a neighborhood kid my age to play with while my father helped out at the funeral home doing small chores. He said it was his way of repaying his cousin for her hospitality. One of the things he did was assist the funeral home's only fulltime employee, Cal Jacobs, move bodies to the visitation room for showing. I asked if he actually touched the dead people, and he said sure, like it was no big deal. Well, it sure was to me. I couldn't imagine doing it.

In our first days there, I had managed to avoid seeing any of the mortuary's clients, but that changed before a week was over. I was walking down the back stairs to meet up with my friend and the door to what I learned was the embalming room was open a bit. As I passed it, Aunt Doris called out to me, inviting me to come in and visit her. Had I known what awaited me, I would have run outside and never looked back. When I entered the room, I was shaken to the core by what I saw—my father's cousin gently, even lovingly, combing the long grey hair of a corpse.

"Isn't she beautiful? So peaceful," she commented, as I stared at her and the body she was all but caressing.

For a moment, I stood in place unable to move forward or to run out of the room, which is what I desperately wanted to do.

"Come over here and see her. This is Mrs. Normandy. Don't be afraid, dear. She's not going to hurt you. She's in heaven now. Look at her lovely face . . . so serene."

As Aunt Doris requested, I finally moved closer. A few feet away from the corpse, I gave it a closer look and had to agree that it did look harmless enough. In fact, it didn't look like what I thought a dead body would. It simply looked like a person sleeping.

"When clients arrive, it's my job to make them appear as they did when they were alive. It's not hard, unless they've been in an accident and have been disfigured. With this sweet lady, all I had to do was give her the beauty shop treatment. You know, do her hair pretty and add some makeup to her face. Here's a picture of her just last month at her birthday party. Doesn't she look about the same?"

"Yes," I said. "Exactly the same."

"Would you like to help me put a little more blush on her cheeks? That's all there is left to do."

"No," I mumbled, horrified by the offer.

The room seemed colder than the rest of the house, but my clenched hands were clammy.

"Can I go play?"

"Of course, dear," answered Aunt Doris, smiling, and I realized she hadn't been serious about my helping her. "The deceased are the most harmless folks in the world, but people think all kinds of horrible things about them," she added, her expression becoming doleful. "It's really a disservice to the departed."

* * *

My new friend, Jeffrey, was really curious about the funeral home and asked all kinds of questions. Mostly he seemed impressed that I actually had the courage to live there.

"Jeez, I would be too afraid. All those dead people inside with you. Aren't you scared?"

"No," I answered, feigning bravery and repeating the words of Aunt Doris. "Dead people are harmless."

"I don't know. They can come back and get you. Sometimes tear your guts out."

"No, they don't. Want to see a dead person?" I said, instantly regretting my impulsive words.

"Really? I've never seen a dead person. I don't know . . . maybe. Well, okay. When?"

"Tomorrow night there's a wake for an old lady. I just saw her. We can go into the visiting room when everybody's left."

We made plans to meet the next day to set up the details of our daring venture. I didn't tell my father about it, because I knew he'd disapprove, thinking it might upset his cousin and possibly endanger our continuing stay. I didn't mind if that happened, because I dreaded being alone in our room at night before my father came to bed. My trepidation about being on my own after sunset further deepened when I asked why his cousin didn't have a husband.

"She did, but he committed suicide down in the basement where the coffins are stored. He was a nice guy but was depressed a lot. Loved to go hunting. Shot himself with one of his rifles, in fact."

"You mean he killed himself right here?"

"About five years ago. Doris was in bad shape after that, but she decided to go it alone, except for Cal. He's worked here for years."

Even at my age, the irony of an undertaker taking his own life in his very own funeral home was not lost on me. The information added to my already towering anxiety, and I resolved never to go near the basement—certain that it housed the late Mr. Roebacker's ghost. Indeed, I was convinced that he was among all the other dead people haunting the place, especially the building's third floor where we slept.

* * *

The next morning, I managed to slip out without being spotted by Aunt Doris and invited back into the embalming room. Jeffrey was at the nearby playground when I arrived, and he rushed to greet me.

"So, we'll actually see a dead person tonight?" asked Jeffrey, excitedly.

"Maybe," I answered tentatively, having reconsidered the plan. "I don't think . . ."

"C'mon, you promised. You can't take it back. If you do, I won't be your friend," pouted Jeffrey.

"I was just kidding. Sure, we'll check out the body after the wake. Meet me outside the funeral home at 8 o'clock, okay? It'll still be light outside. You can come then, right?" I asked, hoping he couldn't. "It's the only time we can see the body."

"You bet. This is going to be so scary, but I want to see a real dead person."

For the remainder of the day, Jeffrey couldn't stop talking about the monster movies he'd seen, particularly the ones where corpses rise out of their coffins and terrorize the living. So by the time we were scheduled to meet for the viewing, I had even more misgivings about the whole idea.

"We better not do this. We could get in trouble if we get caught. Besides, what if the dead person comes back to life," I said, trying to convince Jeffrey that the whole thing was a bad scheme.

"You're just chickening out. If we don't do it, I'm never playing with you again," blurted Jeffrey. "C'mon . . . you said we were going to do it"

With great reluctance, I led him into the main floor of the funeral home. Everything was dimly lit, which only compounded the feeling of entering a forbidden place. At the end of the hallway was the room where bodies were displayed. My heart jumped as I caught sight of part of the coffin. Jeffrey walked behind me, clutching my shoulder.

"You sure you want to see this?" I asked, hoping he had changed his mind.

"Yes," he whispered, his grip on me tightening.

By the time we reached the visitation room, Jeffrey was practically on top of me, and I could tell he was trembling.

"There's the coffin," I said. "Can you see the head?"

At that exact moment, the room was flooded with bright light, and we both let out a loud scream, which added to our distress.

"What are you kids doing in here?" asked Aunt Doris, a sharp edge to her voice.

Neither of us could readily answer as the wind had been sucked from our lungs.

"You're violating this sacred space and being disrespectful to the departed. That is an awful thing to do. Both of you leave right *now*."

It didn't take any convincing for us to comply with Aunt Doris's command. As soon as Jeffrey ran from the house, I went up to my room and waited to be yelled at by my father for what I'd done. But that didn't happen, and I figured his cousin hadn't told him about what had happened. I was thankful for that, but upset when I found that Aunt Doris wouldn't speak to me the next day.

Apparently, what I'd done had soured her on my father as well, and he grew perplexed and then perturbed by her remoteness. It struck me as a good time to press him on our original strategy to hitch a ride west. We had planned to go to California from the start but were waylaid when he went on his latest drunk. It was when he'd finally sobered up that we ended up with his cousin.

"Yeah, that's a good idea," said my father, winking. "It's gotten really dead around here anyway."

By the end of the next day, we were at the Ohio border; a location I felt was probably far enough away to keep the clients of Roebacker's Funeral Home from getting me.

#

Indescribable: A Totally Unsatisfying Short Story

The worst thing imaginable happened as the church bells of St. Mathew's chimed at four o'clock on the 18th of December in 1924. It was a complete shock to the small town's inhabitants and changed how they viewed their lives from that point onward. So catastrophic were its long-term effects that every year on the anniversary of the ghastly incident people flocked to houses of worship worldwide to pray that it would never happen again.

The End

#

Empty Breathing

A mother's influence lasts far beyond her last breath.
—Unknown author

Mrs. Lyle was disconnected from life support, and as her final moments slipped away, she quietly gasped for air.

"It's just a non-cognitive reflex," replied the attending nurse, when Joel asked why his mother was still trying to catch her breath.

"But it looks like she's trying to come around . . . to stay alive."

"I know, Mr. Lyle. We call it Empty Breathing, but they all pretty much do that. She's really gone. I'm sorry. It's very hard to lose a parent," said the nurse, switching off the monitor that displayed a flat red line.

Joel sat beside his mother as her seeming attempts to draw breath gradually subsided and then stopped. A few minutes later, a doctor came into the room and officially pronounced her dead.

"She held on for a long time, Joel. Fought the good fight, as they say. At peace now," he said sympathetically and quickly went on his way.

Mrs. Lyle's grieving son remained in the room until the daylight seeping through the curtains dulled.

"Goodbye, Mother," Joel finally whispered, moving the bed cover over her face the way he'd seen in movies.

When he gave his mother one last glimpse before leaving, he was startled by what he saw. The sheet across her face appeared to be moving up and down. What happened next so flabbergasted Joel, that he fell backwards onto the empty bed next to his mothers.'

"Take this thing off my face, you idiot," demanded the muffled voice from beneath the cover. "Are you trying to kill me? Can't you see I'm breathing, you numbskull? *Non-cognitive reflex*, my ass!"

#

When You Decide You've Had Enough and Want To Take Others With You

Craig Marcus sits alone at a table at the El Fuego Cantina dragging on a Marlboro and taking in fresh air from a portable oxygen tank. The sun is half way down in the New Mexico sky and the plaza is nearly empty because the heat has kept the tourists inside. Across the small patio from him is an elderly couple huddled in the shadow of a *Cinzano* umbrella peering in his direction. When he stares back at them, they turn away abruptly. *Go ahead take a good long look*, he thinks, before deliberately removing the air tubes from his nostrils and placing the fiery tip of his cigarette to their vinyl ends.

#

A Second Opinion

You're not a doctor. Remember that.
No, but I play one on the Internet.
                    —Tracy H. Tucker

Elliot felt he knew things about his health that his primary care physician did not, and this disturbed him. *What if he's missing something?* he wondered, recalling his erratic heartbeat when he hunkered down on the couch. *If he wired me up for an EKG when it did that, it sure wouldn't look normal. How could it? Something has to be wrong with my ticker to do all that fluttering and bouncing around. Maybe I better go to a heart doctor.*

Elliot searched online for a cardiac specialist, deciding not to ask his personal physician for a referral. *He might think I question his ability,* he thought. *It wouldn't be good to give him that idea. It might piss him off, and then who knows how he'd be the next time I see him. These guys don't like to be questioned. They have a God complex.*

After locating a possible cardiologist in his area, Elliot probed the Internet to see how his patients and former patients rated him. *Jeez, the guy is some kind of super doc. Nothing but great comments about him. Wonder if he'll take on new patients? Probably not . . . damn. This dude's a star. His practice has to be closed.*

Despite his doubts, Elliot dialed the specialist's office. To his great surprise, he was told to come in the following week.

By the time the date arrived, Elliot was so filled with a sense of foreboding about the results of his heart exam that he cancelled the appointment. *Probably got nothing wrong with me anyway. After all, my doctor said the EKG looked normal, so why should I doubt him? I'm no expert. Besides the web says it's not uncommon for a heart to sputter and skip beats sometimes,* he reasoned.

153

That evening while Elliot was kicking back and watching MTV, he suddenly realized that his heart was thumping in sync with the latest Juicy J video, and he freaked out.

"Oh, my God, I *hate* him!" he screamed, leaping for the remote.

#

Tastes Like

Provide something that is food for thought at dinner.
It's a good way to distract your guests from your cooking.
                              —Unknown author

Emily Hauser went to the grocery store to do her weekly shopping. When she got there she realized she'd left her list at home. Rather than make the trip back to get it, she figured she'd be able to reconstruct it as she went up and down the aisles.

The first aisle contained International foods, and while she never stopped there, this time she figured she'd check it out. Halfway up the aisle she saw an item that caught her eye. *Headcheese . . . yes,* she thought. Cheese *was* on the list, so she put the package into her cart.

Next she came across something called Mountain Oysters. *My husband loves the shellfish at restaurants. I'll get these for him. A special treat,* Mable decided, placing the can next to the headcheese.

As Emily reached the end of the international food aisle, one last thing caused her to stop because it struck her as particularly interesting. *Looks like a crispy pasta. Hmm . . . "Cambodian delicacy," it says. I'll make a real exotic dinner for Charlie. He'll never expect that,* she thought, carefully setting the packet beside the headcheese and mountain oysters.

The idea of preparing a unique meal for her husband so excited Emily that she decided to cut her shopping short so she could get back home to ready the special feast. At the dining room table, she unveiled her innovative repast with great ceremony.

"*Ta-da!* You always say I feed you the same old thing. So I decided to give you something *very* different."

Starving, her husband enthusiastically dug into the three plates before him.

"Wow, this is delicious. What *is* it?" asked her husband.

"Goat skull, sheep balls, and spider legs," she answered, having Googled the foods when she returned home.

Her husband stared at her in disbelief, his mouth full of the exotic delicacies. After a long pause, he finally he spoke.

"Jeez, honey, the sheep balls are especially tasty."

#

Divine Directives

Everything you can make harsh, you should make harsh.

Everything you can make sweet, you should make sweet.

Everything you can make hurt, you should make hurt.

Everything you can make wise, you should make wise.

Everything you can make fear, you should make fear.

Everything you can make sing, you should make sing.

Everything you can make weep, you should make weep.

Everything you can make envy, you should make envy.

Everything you can make crave, you should make crave.

Everything you can make laugh, you should make laugh.

Everything you can make fail, you should make fail.

Everything you can make bleed, you should make bleed.

Everything you can make heal, you should make heal.

Everything you can make dance, you should make dance.

Everything you can make grieve, you should make grieve.

Everything you can make listen, you should make listen.

Everything you can make love, you should make love.

Everything you can make doubt, you should make doubt.

Everything you can make vicious, you should make vicious.
Everything you can make believe, you should make believe.

"Did I leave anything out, son?" asked God.

#

An Issue of Image

The heavens call to you, and circle about you, displaying to
you their eternal splendors, and your eye gazes only to Earth.
                                        —Dante, 1300

"They'll think we're grotesque creatures given our eight legs
and red protruding eyes. Of course, they look horrible to us
with their pathetically stunted appendages and tiny recessed
optics," said Malin Gota, Commander of the Kaxbar
Planetary Expedition.

"Very true, Malin. And that's why we must approach humans
very carefully to avoid a hostile reaction from them. Certainly
our appearance will provoke them if they're not convinced
that we mean no harm and can benefit their species,"
answered Tekor Mnn, Vice Emperor of Kaxbar.

"They are such an unbeautiful breed and violent as well, but
you think we can help them, Lord Mnn?"

"Of course, from our vastly evolved perspective as
Kaxbarians, they may not appear worth our effort. They are
not a noble genus. Indeed, they are a collection of primitive
warring tribes, but we—members of the Supreme Council—
believe we can lift them from their nascent slime and assist
them to become a more refined life form. Ultimately it will
benefit the universe if we succeed. As you well know,
Commander, that is our sacred purpose with these
expeditions"

"So what is to be done, Vice Emperor?"

"First a series of messages. We'll introduce ourselves through
the various non-visual communication media they have. We
will not show ourselves until we have fully convinced the
Earthlings that we are a force for good—one that wishes to

provide them a better existence. At that point, we'll have explained to them our physical attributes and prepared them to see us as we are."

"We look exactly like the giant mutant spiders in their horror movies. How will they ever get past that, Lord Mnn?"

"We have devised a strategy. First, we will acknowledge having received one of their crude space signals. Our reply will contain a benign greeting indicating a desire to have further contact with them. With each communiqué, we will build a relationship with them designed to diffuse their fear of our physical form when we visit."

"It will be difficult to allay the Earthling's fear of one of the things they find most dreadful—huge spiders.

"Their fear is understandable Malin, because many of their planet's arachnids are venomous and can cause them great harm."

"Actually, only a tiny percentage hurt humans, sir. It is their literature and film that portray them as treacherous vermin. They don't know the truth."

"Well, that will be something we will try to address in our missives, Commander."

* * *

The first interplanetary communiqué sent by the Kaxbarians consisted of a simple acknowledgment of the Earthling's greeting. Rather than the 20 years it took the humans message to reach the alien race, the reply from Kaxbar reached Earth in just two seconds. It was detected by SETI and immediately taken to the White House.

"This has been completely verified?" inquired the president. "There's no mistaking its origin? Totally vetted? No chance of a prank, Dr. Gibbens?"

"No, sir, it is a legitimate message. Every computer program corroborates the coordinates."

"And that is . . .?"

"The Virgo Supercluster, sir."

"Explain."

"It's the closest galaxy to our own. About 42,000 light years away or 25,000 light years from the boundary of our own solar system."

"How did they get a message from us at that distance? How is that possible?"

"We're not sure. Possibly aided by a black hole."

"So this is it? 'Greetings from Kaxbar. We wish to share words of peace with you.' Nothing more?"

"No, sir, not at the moment."

"This situation is not to get beyond these walls, Gibbens. We don't need a panic. When, or if, you get more, let me know immediately."

"Of course, Mr. President."

"By the way, did you respond to the message?"

"Yes, sir. We asked them what words of peace they wished to share."

Four hours after the director of SETI spoke with the President, another message from Kaxbar was received. This one was more detailed:

Dear citizens of planet Earth, it pleases us greatly to have made contact with you. We have had similar contact with many other distant civilizations. Our purpose is to unite the species of the universe as a means of benefitting all. We have advance knowledge in technology and medicine to improve the quality of your lives and we wish to share it with you. But before that is possible, we must convey to you the characteristics of our appearance. We do not look like you. In fact, our appearance will no doubt repel you, but we are not dangerous and do not wish to harm you . . . quite the opposite. It is our objective to provide you with information to make your lives better. So then, allow us to explain why our appearance may, to use a colloquial phrase of yours, freak you out. We have several legs, and they are covered in black follicles. Our torsos rest atop these appendages. Our optic orbs are large and crimson with crosshatching. All three are accompanied by what you would call antennas. These long thin rods serve to detect sound and direct sustenance into our primary consuming orifice, which contain two rows of serrated teeth. The closest thing on your planet that resembles us is your tarantula spider, which we realize most of you find horrifying. We are not predatory and do not possess venom, toxic or otherwise. Please do not fear us because of what we look like. We know your planet does define objects by their appearance, but we ask that you transcend your disdain of arachnids, or things that appear like them, so we may come together in harmony and peace. We have so much good to share with you— information that will eliminate a great many of your physical ills and provide you with enhanced happiness.

Two repetitions of the communiqué were received within minutes of each other.

* * *

"Holy crap!" exclaimed the president, upon listening to the Kaxbarian's message. "They sound hideous looking."

"Yes, sir, but we believe they are sincere about contributing to the betterment of humanity."

"So you recommend inviting them, Gibbens?"

"Mr. President, this could change everything. Imagine if they could cure cancer and eliminate famine and drought. California has become a dustbowl and the world is experiencing more conflict than ever. They could relieve these woes and allow us to progress as a species."

"Other countries are of the same thinking, and want them to come. But what if they are hostiles? What then?"

"Every indication so far is that they are a magnanimous presence with altruistic intentions. We stand to benefit from them in countless ways . . . if we trust them. We believe they possess many solutions and answers we have long sought."

"You act as if they're the second coming of God."

"They could be just that, sir. Here to put us back on course. To provide us salvation."

"Now, don't get all religious on me, Gibbens. Okay, tell them we await their arrival. Find out when that will be. We need to brace the public for what it is about to see . . . giant benevolent spiders. Shit, why couldn't they look like Brad Pitt or Angelina Jolie, or a combination of the two?"

* * *

SETI sent an invitation to the Kaxbarians advising them to come on the 26th of the following month, giving the governments of the planet time to assure their citizens that the tarantula-appearing extraterrestrials were coming in peace with great gifts for the human race. Every hour of every day, announcements were transmitted over all media, advising people not to be frightened by the alien's appearance.

The Kaxbarians were directed to land their craft on the historic Washington Mall, and at noon on the date of their designated arrival, the sky was filled with a number of foreign objects. The largest of them touched down in front of the Lincoln Memorial as the world watched on all manner of digitized screens. The streets around the landing site had been cordoned off to keep crowds away. Only the U.S. President and high officials of the planet's foremost governments formed the official greeting party.

"Jesus, this is it. We're really making contact with an intelligent life form from another heavenly body. Look at their spaceship. It's covered with piece symbols . . . amazing!" observed the president to his uneasy staff.

"It reminds me of the movie *The Day the Earth Stood Still*," commented the vice president.

"Except we're about to see giant spiders. I'd prefer Michael Rennie in his Tin Man outfit," quipped the president.

Shortly after the Kaxbarian ship landed, its portal opened and Commander Gota began to crawl down the ramp.

The gasp coming from the awaiting crowd of dignitaries was loud, and it caused the emissary from the Virgo Galaxy to stop its descent.

"Okay, we knew what they'd look like," said the president, reassuringly. "Stay cool. We'll take care of this."

As the Kaxbarian leader approached, a shot rang out. In the confusion that followed, the alien ship lifted off, leaving the body of the fallen victim in its swirling wake.

"What a wicked *web* we weave," snickered the vice president.

"That's a good one," chuckled the president.

#

The Substance of Nothing

"There's no afterlife," declared Sarah. "When we die . . . we simply *die*. That's it, *period*. We're caput. It's the end of the road . . . *fini.*"

"Yeah," agreed Emil. "There's no heaven or hell. We don't *go* anywhere. We just enter the void"

"What's a *void?*" asked 11 year old Linda."

"It's *nothingness*," answered Sarah.

After a period of careful thought, Linda replied. "Well, if there *is* nothingness, then there *is* something . . . right?"

Neither adult responded.

#

Cold Girl

I've never been crazy. I'm a very good girl, to be
honest. I don't do anything to hurt anybody.
—Leighton Meester

So I'm heading home after running a few errands and I come
to a red light. In front of me is this shiny white Mercedes.
Looks brand new to me. I see the back of the driver's head
and notice she has a cellphone pressed against the blond
locks that hang over her left ear. Damn, what is it with
women and phones? Strikes me that every other female driver
is on her cellphone. What's so important that they have to
jeopardize everyone's life when they're behind the wheel?

So the light changes to green, but she doesn't move. Just
keeps yapping away like she's sitting in her living room.
"C'mon," I grumble, and then hit my horn. Bitch still doesn't
move. Finally, as I'm about to flip her the bird, she hits the
gas and speeds off, taking a wider turn than she should at the
intersection.

I notice that her window is wide open, which strikes me as
pretty nuts since it's in the freakin' 20s outside. I expect her
to close it, but she doesn't. My eyes catch her license plate as
she pulls away from me: "CLDGRL." *Vanity plates are common*
on luxury cars, I think, trying to decipher the letters. "Call
Girl?" Nope. "Calendar Girl?' Maybe.

Ahead of us is another red light, and I catch up to her car.
She's still on her frigging cell. "Dumb, rich broad," I growl.
And then the light changes. This time she doesn't play
zombie and takes a left right away after it turns green. That
happens to be in the direction I'm heading. *Is she a neighbor?* I
wonder, and figure no way driving that $100K beauty.   She
still has her window open. *Jesus, she must be some cold blooded girl,*
I think, and then the meaning of the license plate's letters

dawns on me: *Cold Girl!* That's it, and boy is that on the money.

Suddenly she slows to a near crawl. *What the hell is that about?* I ask myself. *Goddamn it, she's still flapping on her cell. Totally fucking oblivious to me behind her.* I can't pass her because there's a solid line between the lanes on the two-way and cars keep coming from the opposite direction anyway.

Now she's totally stopped and there's no light or stop sign. I'm on her bumper. *What* is *going on with her?* I wonder and hit my horn several times, finally just lying on the sucker. She looks in her rearview mirror for the very first time, and I catch her dark eyes peering back at me. They have this real mean look in them.

"So move, you douche bag!" I blurt, hoping she can read my lips. Then I open my window and give her the bird, moving my hand up and down to make it even more obscene. She still doesn't move, and I've had it. "Son of a bitch!" I shout at the top of my lungs and get out of my car.

As I approach her hotsy-totsy vehicle, she jumps from it and comes at me with a tire iron in her right hand. Next thing I know, I'm on the ground and everything goes black. When I wake up at a hospital, the cop who's been questioning me says he checked at the motor registry and there's no plate that matches the one I gave him.

Now what the hell am I suppose to think? *I know what I saw, and that was some ice lady back there, all right.* When I'm released from the ER, the cops give me a ride to my car that's parked near the spot where I was attacked. They ask again if I'm up to driving home, and I say I'm fine. "Go slow," they say, and I thank them.

My head is still throbbing when I pull out of the Walgreen's parking lot, but I'm thankful I didn't have a severe concussion. The ER doc was surprised I only ended up with a big lump on the side of my noggin. He says I should have had a cracked skull. Guess I'm as hard headed as they say.

Now I'm only a block away from the intersection where that crazy broad was stopped at the light and who pulls in front of me? *Jesus H. Christ!* No, really, it's the fucking white Mercedes with the "CLDGRL" license plate! I have no idea what to do as we stop for a red light. So I just let her drive away after the light has gone through two changes.

I'll be damned if I'll get on Cold Girl's case again, I tell myself and wait until her car is out of sight. But when I get to the next intersection, she is waiting for me. This time she stays her ground refusing to move despite the light changing a dozen times. I wonder why the cars behind me aren't freaking out and then see that the one to my rear is the same as the one in front of me. In fact, all the cars behind it are exactly the same as far as my eyes can see.

Panic overtakes me, and I can't move. Then I start screaming uncontrollably as the crazy driver in front of me leaves her car and walks in my direction. I shut my eyes and ready myself for another attack but none occurs. There's a muffled voice coming from outside my car window asking what's the matter, and when I dare to look, it turns out to be the cop who took me to my car just a short while ago. He says my head injury must be worse than thought and instructs me to get out and come with him.

We don't get far, however, because the girl in the white Mercedes with the CLDGRL license plate comes up behind the cop like a phantom and hits him with her tire iron. Then she looks at me and howls like a banshee.

"Stop following me, asshole!"

#

My Dear Old Dad

I see all the last photos of aged and ailing men posted on Facebook in tribute on Father's Day and think that if my loved ones do that to me I'll come back to haunt them.

#

Brett's Voice

Things are never as scary when you've
got a best friend.
                        —Bill Watterson

I've had this voice in my head since I was an adolescent . . .
16 years old, to be exact. At first I was frightened by it. I
thought someone must be in my bedroom. But after a close
search, I found no one, which led me to think that my room
might be occupied by a ghost or spirit of some kind. The first
thing the voice said to me took the form of a question: "Why
are you afraid to ask Kara to go on a date?" Without thinking,
I answered. "She'd never say yes." As soon as I spoke, I
realized something amazing had happened.

I'm 24 now, and the voice has been with me ever since, and
I'm thankful for it. By that I mean it has always given me
good advice. In the beginning, I thought I was going crazy
and wondered if I should tell someone about what was going
on. But then I realized everything the voice told me to do
turned out fine . . . *great,* in fact.

At the advice of the voice—which I named Brett, because I
always liked that name—I did ask Kara out. She said yes after
I spread the rumor that the guy she liked was seeing another
girl. Brett gave me that idea, and it worked out better than I
ever thought. We went out a few more times until Kara got
back together with her old boyfriend. By then I didn't care,
because I liked another girl better. The voice helped me get
her, too.

On senior prom night, Brett suggested that I put a laxative in
the punch bowl as a joke. I was kind of pissed at my fellow
seniors for treating me like I wasn't as good as them. So I got
a strong one and slipped it in the bowl when nobody was
watching. Later in the evening, it seemed that everyone was

lining up at the bathrooms. Some kids didn't make it and you can imagine what happened to them. It was hysterical, especially because Kara and her boyfriend ran outside and crapped in the parking lot. They didn't see me, but I followed them. While they were relieving themselves, they were groaning like sick cows. I almost pissed my pants laughing.

College wasn't easy for me, especially the math and science courses. I was on the path to failing my first year, but Brett came to the rescue. He told me where to sit so I could see the tests of the smartest kids in the classes that were giving me the most trouble. I copied their answers and ended up with a B in geometry and an A- in natural sciences. That actually put me on the honor roll. Brett helped me throughout college, and when I graduated, my parents couldn't have been more proud.

My first job was also thanks to Brett's assistance. He suggested I beef up my resume a little by adding a few things—nothing huge, really. Put myself down as an assistant manager at the burger joint I worked for two summers. Say I was coordinator of the debate team, even though I was only on it for one semester. Beef up my college GPA a bit, despite the fact that I already had a 3.2. Just a few minor embellishments, but they must have made a difference because I got the first job I applied for. Brett, you're the *man!*

Three years later, when I got promoted to regional sales director, I was given my own secretary. She was just out of Katherine Gibbs and very nervous. She wasn't the strongest candidate for the job, but I hired her because she was a hot little babe. I treated her with patience and understanding as she got settled in and gained her confidence. She was sweet and very naïve, and things quickly got to the point that I wanted to have sex with her more than anything. So I began to make some moves.

At first, she seemed confused by my advances, but Brett gave me some great pointers to keep her from getting scared or upset. Eventually, it became clear that she was becoming attracted to me. Then I went for it, and kissed her, moving my hands over her taut body. Soon I had her on my office couch, and we were having passionate sex. We did this many more times, and then she got serious, wanting to know where it was leading. Brett told me to dump her at that point—and I did.

As time went on, I continued on my path to business success. Gaining clients was easy with Brett's direction. He told me to promise anything that would get them to sign the bottom line, and that's what I did. Once I put the close on them, I could deal from a position of strength, said Brett. His rule was simple and on the mark, I thought: "A bird in the hand is better than two in the bushes, because you can squeeze the one in your hand until it goes along with what you want." I did a lot of squeezing and made heaps of money as a result. Not long after, I was promoted to national director of sales. Thanks, Brett. Love you, guy.

When Melinda came into my life, I was blown away by her beauty and intelligence, not to mention the fact that she came from a wealthy family. It took me a while to woo her, but she eventually said yes to my marriage proposal. Brett had vetted me carefully during the courtship process. He knew I had to have her as my wife, so he constantly told me how to act and what to say.

It was obvious from the start that she wanted children, although I had no interest in that whatsoever. Brett told me to pretend that I was in order to consummate the deal, so I did. Before we tied the knot, I got a vasectomy and the kid thing was off the table, unbeknownst to Melinda. We stayed together until I refused to have a fertility test, and then she asked for a divorce. By then, I was tired of our relationship anyway, so once again moving on seemed the right thing to do.

Coming home late at night from my 45th birthday party—where I had over-imbibed, as usual—I hit a cyclist. I pulled over with the purpose of checking on the person, but Brett told me to keep going. His advice had always been right, but for some reason I couldn't leave the victim alone. "Drive on . . . drive on!" demanded the voice, as I got out of my car. "Why aren't you listening to me? What are you doing?"

The person I had struck appeared to have no pulse, and I dialed 911. Within minutes after the police arrived and determined the person was dead, I was charged with driving under the influence resulting in vehicular homicide. Five weeks later, I was sentenced to 6 years at a medium-security prison. In my dreary cell, I pleaded for Brett to come back. I had not heard from him since the accident. It was the first time in nearly 30 years that he hadn't spoken to me on a daily basis. He had been my closest friend, and without his companionship, I felt abandoned and despondent.

After four-and-a-half years, I was released due to good behavior, and that's when Brett returned. I had mixed feelings about him by that time. Why had he left me in my greatest time of need, I asked?

"Because you disobeyed me, you stupid bastard, and look what that got you," he answered, adding, "I'm more than just some damn voice in your head."

"I know that, Brett. You're so much more than just that."

He was right, of course. By not listening to him I had suffered dearly.

"Please stay!" I pleaded.

"And if I do, you'll always do as I say?"

"Yes." I said. "*Always.*"

#

After Admitting That He'd Slept With Her Sister

The last thing Kyle recalled was tumbling down the rocky slope and seeing the look of satisfaction on his wife's face as it grew smaller.

#

The Pictures on Dorian's Computer

Isn't that the most perverse thing you've ever seen?
—John Waters

That Dorian Wilder possessed an extreme penchant for the macabre was clear. Why that was the case, especially given his seemingly bucolic childhood, was the question. But whatever disgusting and hideous things he could find on the Internet (and there was no shortage) excited and aroused him. He avidly searched for images of assaults, murders, explosions, car accidents, and bloody fights, but nothing pleased him more than videos or pictures of disfigured faces. His obsession had first been piqued as an adolescent when he came upon a picture of Joseph Carey Merrick—the so-called Elephant Man of the 19th century. This so intrigued and captivated his imagination that in the next few years he amassed a vast digital archive of grossly deformed countenances.

By the time Dorian reached full adulthood, his photo collection probably numbered in the thousands—he didn't know exactly. He had managed to plumb the depths of depravity and ferret out things he'd never known or even imagined existed. Among his gallery of grotesqueries were individuals with Leprosy riven skin, burn victims melted beyond recognition, and mutilated heads smashed to a gooey pulp. When he attempted to engage friends with his hobby, their appalled reactions quickly convinced him to keep it private. *They just don't appreciate the unique aesthetics these pictures contain,* he told himself. *They can't get beyond the surface and see the true beauty to be found there.*

After nearly seven years with the same iMac, Dorian was forced to replace it with a new model, and this is when his all-consuming avocation took an unwelcome turn. His arcane files of gnarled and disfigured faces would not transfer to a memory stick no matter how many times he tried. He considered forwarding them to his work computer for backup, but then decided not to in the off chance they might be accessed by his employer. Finally, he decided to buy the new computer and transfer his special files to it directly, hoping nothing would happen in the process that might cause him to loose his cherished digital repository. However, once again, the files would not budge from the old computer.

In the end, Dorian gave up trying to relocate his prized photos and decided to keep them on his old machine. Despite its age and growing dilapidation, he still could access the files without encountering major problems. He would continue gathering his favorite images on his new computer and keep his old iMac in a small cubicle in his apartment he'd been using as a catch all for his neglected exercise equipment.

When he unplugged his old computer to move it, however, he was surprised that it did not power down. In fact, it defaulted to a selfie of him that he'd taken just the day before. *What's going on?* he mumbled, pushing the computer's off button several times. *Got a mind of your own, eh? Okay, let's take you to your new space, old boy.* Dorian placed it on a small table in the nook and returned to the task of setting up his new iMac. As soon as it was readied, he renewed the never-ending search for more examples of his favorite subject. Before long, the archive on his replacement computer was so substantial that he had all but forgotten about his previous cache of lurid photos.

* * *

Several weeks passed, and Dorian decided to take a trip down memory lane and revisit his older images, he was startled to find the elder computer still fired up with his picture on the monitor. He checked the electrical chord and then realized he had never plugged it into the outlet. *How can this be? Where can it be getting its power?* he wondered. When he looked at his face on the screen, he sensed that something was not quite right. Then he noticed a slight droop to his eyelids. *I look like I'm about to fall to sleep. That's not how the selfie was.*

After an hour of scrolling through his old photo archive, he attempted to shut down the computer, but as before it resisted his efforts. When he rose to leave, he was jarred by the reappearance of his selfie without having accessed it. This time, his lids covered most of his eyes, leaving just a slit of sclera visible. *Damn, what the hey with that?* He felt a ripple of chills on his back as he shut the door to the alcove and went for his cellphone. A mix of relief and apprehension filled him when his selfie looked as it had when he first snapped it. He then checked his reflection in a mirror and was satisfied by what he saw. *Okay, that old computer is just glitching out. What else could it be?* he asked himself. *I'll check it again tomorrow.*

When, several days later, Dorian finally did return to his former computer, he was appalled at what had become of his own image on the monitor. His cheeks were hollowed out and his skin was discolored and riddled with small red veins. *No, what the . . .? Someone has to be screwing with me, but who? Nobody has been in my house. Maybe I'll just get rid of this frigging thing. Smash the screen and dump it.*

He resolved to destroy the old computer but then thought of the irreplaceable image files it contained and decided against it. *Just don't look at the selfie. Pretend it's not there. Go right to the files. Keep your eyes averted*, he told himself and did not return to the old iMac for a month. By that time, he had amassed a formidable file of hideous visions on his replacement computer that rivaled those on his old one. Yet, there were numerous images in the original file that he could not resist revisiting, so eventually he returned to the storeroom that housed his out-of-date processor without looking at his mutating selfie.

Keep your head down. Call up the photo file without looking at the monitor. Wait until you're certain it's gone. Just look at the corner of the screen until you know it's changed. He clicked the necessary link and when the screen flickered as it does when it goes to another location, he looked up.

"God!" he yelped, encountering the most horrible rendition of any face he had ever seen . . . and this one was *his*. It was a virtual composite of everything odious that could possibly befall a human physiognomy. *It's awful. Jesus, no . . . it can't be real,* he mumbled, turning away from the screen in revulsion and horror. *It's the most ravaged face I've ever seen, and it's* mine. *Impossible. What the hell is happening?*

After several moments pondering the situation, Dorian slowly turned back to the screen and stared at it. Gradually, the anguish he felt changed into sublime satisfaction, and his lips were stretched to their outer most limits by a broad smile. *Yes,* he thought, feeling mounting joy. *Yes . . . this is the best one ever. It's fucking wonderful.*

#

The Intransitive

Eugene Salisbury had his office moved three times, and when it was announced that he would have to move yet again, he confronted his boss.

"Why do I have to move again?" he inquired.

To which his boss replied, "Excuse me, but who are you anyway?"

"You mean you don't even know who I am?" asked Eugene.

"Well, how could I? Every time I come to your office, there's someone different there."

#

Hair Today

We're all born bald, baby.
        —Telly Savalas

I look in the mirror and see a somewhat older guy with a decent head of hair. Of course, years ago it was really thick and wavy . . . and dark brown. Really enviable crop up there back then, but not so bad now either, I think. And then a friend calls me baldy.

"Huh? What the hell do you mean? You're the bald one. Not me," I growl, reaching for the back of my head where I know my hair has gotten a little thinner.

He chuckles at my response and crinkles his brow as if he knows something that I don't. I'm still pissed at his remark, and I tell him that his forehead has pushed his hairline to the back of his neck. He's suddenly less amused than he was.

"Yeah, well your bald spot looks like Oklahoma," he counters.

"What the hell does that even mean?" I ask, ready to launch a counteroffensive.

"It means," says he, "that you got wide open spaces back there."

My blood pressure is rising as I shoot at his bow rather than over it.

"You have so little hair left that a comb over wouldn't cover anything."

My salvo is followed by a long awkward silence, which is finally broken by our female colleague.

"Hey, you two cue balls, want to have lunch today?" she says in her usual wise-ass manner.

"Sure," we reply, giving one another a hard look.

#

Rising To the Occasion

I am told he makes a handsome corpse, and becomes
his coffin prodigiously.

—Oliver Goldsmith

When Stubby Layman read that a funeral home in New Orleans was displaying corpses outside of caskets in seated positions, he took keen notice. *That's the way I want to be shown. Nobody gets to look down on you that way. People been looking down at me my whole life. Can't help it if I'm short. I'll be damned if they'll look down on me at my own funeral!*

Stubby immediately called the funeral home he'd chosen to handle his remains. For seven years, he'd battled leukemia and now his demise was very close at hand according to his doctors.

"Yes, Mr. Layman. We learned about the new client presentations at our recent funeral director's convention in New Orleans. We also saw the article and read it with special interest. We certainly can accommodate your wishes. Can you tell us what sitting position you'd prefer: cross-legged, parallel-legged, slightly reclining? Kneeling is also an option. Like in the prayer position. Very touching. And what would you like to be seated on . . . that is, if you're not kneeling? The choices are really up to you," said undertaker, Carl Bellowski.

"Oh . . . I hadn't really thought of that. Lots to think about. I sure want it to be right. I'll get back to you, okay?"

"Certainly. Your *last* wishes are Bellowski's *first* objective."

Stubby had heard that line a number of times since contacting the funeral home and had quickly developed an aversion to it.

They sound like a damn used car dealership, he thought, hanging the phone up.

* * *

For the next couple of days, Stubby considered a variety of positions and venues. His first idea was to appear in full monarch regalia in the lavish leather recliner he'd impulsively purchased a year earlier. *I'll get some more use out of that pricy La-Z-Boy before it goes to the Salvation Army.* It wasn't long before he had another idea. *Could get them to put me behind the wheel in one of those tiny Smart Cars and invite people to sit next to me in the passenger seat. If ever there was a road coffin, that's it.*

The idea that he finally settled on came to him while he was lying in bed unable to sleep—he'd be sitting at a folding card table playing gin rummy. For a dozen years, Stubby participated in a weekly card game with his closest friends, Howie, Sam, and Don. It had been the high point of his week, because living alone as he did left him craving companionship. His job as a supply clerk for a metal fastener company afforded him little contact with people, so getting together with his longtime buddies was a singular pleasure.

The only thing that occasionally tarnished his enjoyment at the gatherings was the ribbing he got because of rarely having a winning hand. He figured it was a small price to pay for the joy he derived from the weekly events. So he took the taunting in seeming stride, concealing the mild annoyance it caused him.

"Hey, it's my strategy to let you guys win, and it's working perfectly."

When he thought about the Saturday night conclaves, he knew that being displayed at a card table was the perfect way

186

to bid his friends farewell. *Maybe I can embellish the scene,* he snickered, amused by yet another idea.

"I believe we can do that, Mr. Layman. It'll take some thought, but as you know our client's *last* wishes are Bellowski's *first* objective."

"I do. I do. Thank you. I'll come by next week to help you work it out, Mr. Bellowski," said Stubby, with a mischievous glint in his eye.

* * *

Stubby spent the last week of his life at a hospice, and when he passed, his body was delivered to Bellowski's to *sit* in state. As they had planned, he was placed at a table and playing cards were put in his hands. When the small group of attendees arrived for the wake, they were seated before a black velvet curtain behind which their deceased friend waited.

Howie, Sam, and Don sat together in the front row and wondered about the unusual setup. They had expected to view their friend in the customary fashion.

"The coffin is probably behind the curtain," speculated Don.

"Never seen it done like this," said Howie.

"I *won't* have what's behind curtain number one," joked Sam, causing his comrades to chuckle.

They squelched their inappropriate mirth when Mr. Bellowski appeared.

"Welcome, ladies and gentleman. Thank you for coming to pay your respects to the dearly departed. Mr. Layman has chosen a novel way to exit the world. As you may or more than likely may *not* know, there's a new trend in the presentation of the deceased, and Mr. Layman has chosen to bid you goodbye in a somewhat unconventional fashion. Nonetheless, it is the way he wished to say farewell. Here at Bellowski's a clients *last* wishes are our *first* objective."

With that, the funeral director pulled the curtain aside to reveal Stubby at the card table. The mourners gasped at the first sight of the seated cadaver.

"Jesus, you see what he's doing?" gulped Howie.

Just as the attendees were trying to come to terms with the scene before them, Stubby's right arm bolted upward, causing them to gasp again. But what followed prompted everyone, including Stubby's former Saturday night card game chums, to leap from their chairs and dash for the exit.

"Rummy!" shouted the prerecorded voice of Stubby Layman. "I win, you bastards!"

Afterwards, when Carl Bellowski placed Stubby into his casket, he was certain his client's expression had changed from what he had sculpted. It was never his technique to shape a cadaver's lips into a broad grin.

#

I'm Still Substance. Don't I Matter?

There remains something of me in the box. Come visit.

#

That House

*[Boy] your head is haunted; you have wheels
in your head! You imagine things . . .*
— Max Stirner

The pale blue house with the gambrel roof at 31 Coyle Street
sat at the far end of an immense treeless lawn seemingly big
enough to accommodate a football field. Spruce trees rose
behind the house like rockets set to launch. It struck 12 year-
old Brendan Quinn as the loneliest-looking house he'd ever
seen. His perspective was compounded by the fact that he'd
never noticed a single soul around the solitary dwelling. It
seemed as if the place had been abandoned, except that it was
well maintained. Its shrubs were always neatly trimmed and
bright flowers filled its window boxes.

On one occasion, Brendan had dared to check its mailbox
and found it empty. *Someone was getting the mail, unless none was
being delivered.* He was convinced that the differently shaped
structure—his neighborhood consisted almost exclusively of
raised ranches and capes—was occupied, if not by humans,
then maybe by ghosts. Someone or something lived there, he
concluded. But who or what, he regularly wondered, as he
passed it on his way to and from school.

"Mom, who lives in the house with the big lawn in front of
it?" asked Brendan.

"What house are you talking about, honey? On our street?"

"Yes. It's number 31. You know, the blue one down there
with the weird roof," said Brendan, pointing behind him.

"Oh, *that* house. I think there's an elderly couple there . . . the
Gastons, I believe. They've lived there forever. Long before
we moved here. Why?"

"Just wondering. I never see anybody there. It looks so lonely."

"*Lonely?* That's an interesting way to put it. They probably never go out, Brendan."

"Maybe they died."

"No, I don't think so, sweetie. We would have heard. When you're their age, you don't venture far."

* * *

Despite that reasonable supposition, Brendan's fascination with the house grew. He felt drawn to it for some inexplicable reason and spent long stretches of time just watching it in the hope of sighting its occupants. The house even made occasional appearances in his dreams, and he'd wake up feeling unsettled. On weekends, Brendan would stroll by it with binoculars for a closer look inside, but there was never anything to see other than a large picture on the wall that hung above a gold couch. It depicted a tree full of black birds . . . or maybe bats, he thought.

Walking to school on a snowy late November day, it occurred to Brendan that while everything had turned brown and barren, due to the deepening winter, the flowers in the gambrel's window boxes remained bright and fresh looking.

"You know, Mom, there's still flowers at the Gaston's house."

"Huh?"

"Yeah, they're under their windows and really pretty. How come?"

"Well, they're probably artificial, honey. When you get their age, gardening gets difficult."

"They don't look artificial."

"They'd have to be. Flowers couldn't exist in this weather."

Brendan resolved to check them out and on his way to school the next morning, he crept up to a window box for a closer look. When he reached the house, he peered inside and was surprised to see the tree painting no longer held countless black birds. *They're gone,* he thought, *how can that be? The birds were there. I know they were there.* He felt an icy shiver move up his spine.

Finally, he directed his gaze to the window box. *They look alive,* he thought, and touched the petal of a bright orange marigold. It was soft and supple. *They* are *real. They're not artificial. Mom won't believe it.*

Suddenly, he was struck by an irresistible urge to knock on the door. He wanted, needed, to make contact with whoever lived in the house once and for all. His heart racing, he clacked the gold knocker on the front door several times. When it finally opened, he was pulled inside with such force that his neck snapped.

* * *

When her son had not appeared home from school over an hour after he usually did, Brendan's mother began to worry. By the time her husband got home from work, she was beside herself with concern for her absent child.

"He probably went to Jamie's house. He does that sometimes," said Frank Quinn, trying to assuage his wife's rising anxiety.

"No, I called Jamie's house, and Brendan wasn't there."

"He'll show up. Give him another hour."

But two hours later, Brendan had not appeared, and the Quinn's scoured the neighborhood for him in their car.

"There's that Gaston house down the road. Brendan was obsessed with it. Maybe we should check it out," suggested Casey Quinn.

"No, we can't bother them. They're old. What would they know? Brendan wouldn't be there, babe."

After another hour passed without any results in their search for Brendan, Frank called the police and reported his son missing.

Twenty minutes later, Sheriff Maynard was at their house. Two very anxious parents greeted him.

"He never does this. We've checked with everybody, and nobody's seen him. Something happened," said Casey, gulping back tears.

"Has he behaved differently in recent days? Anything out of the ordinary?" inquired the officer.

"No, not that I've noticed," replied Frank.

"Well, there is one thing. He's been fixated on the Gaston's place. He was curious because he never saw them there. Thought the house was empty. Maybe haunted or something. Just a kid's imagination, I guess, but maybe you could question them?"

Of course we will, and everybody else around here. I've got a deputy on it already, and I'm getting on it, too. I'll keep in touch. Don't worry. Kids usually show up."

* * *

Sheriff Maynard parked in front of the Gaston's house and ate the fried chicken his wife had packed for him when he was called away to investigate Brendan's disappearance. *Why the hell would a kid be in there with those old fogies?* he thought. When he finished his postponed meal, he approached the house and knocked on its front door.

"Hello, Mr. Gaston," said Sheriff Maynard, when the door swung open.

"Oh, Sheriff, is there a problem?"

"Yes, the Quinn boy from up the street is missing, so we're checking to see if anybody in the neighborhood has seen him."

"Sorry, no. We don't get out much."

Sheriff Maynard was struck with how robust the octogenarian before him appeared.

"My . . . you're looking great for your . . .. Have you found the fountain of youth, Mr. Gaston? What's your secret?"

"Thank you. No secret, really. We have a mini-gym in the basement, with a treadmill and stationary bike. Don't miss a day down there."

"Well, hello Mrs. Gaston," said Maynard, as a small woman looking younger than he recalled appeared at her husband's

194

side. "Wow, the two of you really are the poster seniors for good health."

"We do our best to stay fit, sheriff. Mr. Gaston makes sure of that, don't you, dear?"

"It's sure working for you folks. Jeez, you don't look that much older than me. I turned 60 last month. Course, I'd look better without this gut," said Maynard, clutching his bulging mid-drift.

The Gastons made no further comment, and the sheriff bid them goodbye.

"If you see the Quinn boy, please let me know."

* * *

Several days passed and Brendan remained unfound, despite the considerable efforts to find him by all the available members of the sheriff's department and several community volunteers. Meanwhile, Casey Quinn's suspicions about the Gastons had grown. *They know something. Maybe they're keeping him captive in their house for some perverse reason,* she thought. *Brendan knew something wasn't right there. That's why he was so drawn to that house. He had a premonition.* Again, she asked Maynard to search the Gaston's house, and it was with great reluctance that he agreed to do so.

"They're nice old people. Don't think they'd hurt a fly. But if you insist, I'll go over."

"Please look closely, sheriff. Check every room."

Maynard complied with the distraught mother's wishes, inspecting every corner of the Gaston's house.

"Sorry, Mrs. Quinn, but there wasn't any sign that Brendan had ever been in their house. They were more than willing to let me look into all their closets and their basement and attic. Even checked their shed. Was embarrassed to do that to those folks, but they were very gracious about it."

"What about the girl who vanished from the neighborhood 28 years ago, sheriff?" asked Mr. Quinn.

"What girl, Frank? There was another child from here that disappeared? You didn't tell me."

"I just learned about it a couple days ago from Gil at the Texaco station. He mentioned it, and I checked it out. The girl was 13 years old. She lived the next street over. They never found her."

"Why didn't you tell me, Frank?"

"I thought it would just make things worse if you knew. I should have . . ."

"You knew, too. Didn't you sheriff?"

"Sorry, I just didn't want to add to your woes, and it was so long ago. Can't be any connection . . . believe me"

"How do you know that?" blurted Casey, abruptly leaving from the room.

There's a child killer in this neighborhood, she thought, while starring at herself in the bathroom mirror, *and I'll find him . . . or* them.

* * *

Just as her son had done, Casey took up a vigil on the road in front of the blue gambrel. Each day she spent time gazing at the house for any sign of movement from within or without. This she did to the chagrin of her husband.

"Please, Casey. You can't do that. The neighbors understand what you're . . . *we're* going through, but they'll think you've gone over the edge. What you're doing is called *stalking*. The Gastons could file charges against you. Get a restraining order," said Frank Quinn.

"Let them. I'd like that!" snapped Casey, who continued her surveillance as the days and weeks passed.

Finally, on an early spring morning, she rose from bed having decided to confront the occupants of 31 Coyle Street herself. She would demand to search the house and do so even if they objected. Casey stepped up to the door and clacked the knocker as hard as she could.

"Yes, can I help you?" responded a familiar looking middle-aged man."

Casey was momentarily at a loss for words. *Who is this? This isn't . . . But he . . .*

"Is there something I can do for you, Miss?"

"Is Mr. Gaston here?"

"I'm Mr. Gaston?"

"No, I mean the old . . . "

"Oh, my father?"

"*Your* father? I guess."

"I'm sorry. My parents moved to Florida to get away from the cold. My wife and me moved in. It's all worked out quite nicely. We really love this house."

There was something very off-putting about the young Gaston's expression, and Casey's resolve began to waver. Nonetheless, she managed to forge ahead with her plan.

"Would you mind if I looked through your house?"

"Why? Oh, . . . you're the mother of the boy who's missing?"

Yes, my son was . . . *is* Brendan Quinn."

"You know, I *would* mind. You had the police bother my poor parents about this. I'm sorry about your son, but that has nothing to do with us. Good day."

Casey stood before the shut door for a moment and then walked slowly down the long driveway to the street. Suddenly, she experienced a strong feeling that she was being watched. When she reached the street, she turned and peered back at the house.

It seemed utterly devoid of life. The words of her son echoed through her head:

It looks so lonely, Mom.

#

Something In Reserve

Avery Collins and his fellow climber, Jason Mortimer, had reached Camp 3 on Mt. Everest. It had been a particularly grueling ascent from the previous level, and it was clear that the two middle-age men were spent. After a prolonged silence, Collins turned to his cohort and spoke.

"Should we . . .?" he asked tentatively.

"I suppose . . . Yes, I think we should," answered Mortimer.

A second later both men leapt from the ledge on which they'd been huddling. Not more than a few feet in the air, they spread their wings. Back at Base Camp, Collins turned to Mortimer and mumbled unhappily

"I thought we were only going to do that as a *last* resort."

#

Intimate Apparel Thieves From Outer Space

Everyone's quick to blame the alien.

—Aeschylus

Agnes was returning from shopping when she noticed something odd hovering over her house. At first she thought it was a large bird, but then she realized it had no wings. *How can something fly without wings?* she asked herself, taking a closer look. It wasn't until she reached the walkway leading to the front door of her townhouse condo that it became clear to her that it was a UFO. A metal platform extended from it to her second floor bedroom. "Oh no!" she blurted and ran into her house and up the stairs. As soon as she reached her bedroom, she threw the door open and stepped in. A blinding light greeted her, causing her to freeze in her tracks. When the light faded, she surveyed her surroundings. Everything looked in order and the object that had been outside of the window had vanished. It wasn't until two days later as Agnes was preparing for a party that she noticed her cherished *Star Trek* faux fur rabbits-foot pasties were missing. Furious at finding them gone, she went to the window, opened it, and shrieked toward the heavens. "YOU FUCKERS BRING THOSE NIPPLE COVERS BACK!"

#

Just An *Old* Cowhand

There are lots of people who mistake their
imagination for their memory.
                    —Josh Billings

Billy-John Calhoun saddled up his horse, Rickets, in the corral of his windblown homestead north of Ashby, Nebraska, and rode it westward with great purpose. It took him just over a half an hour to reach the tiny farming town of Bingham. He kept a gallop through the two-block center as he moved in the direction of Ellsworth, some 15 miles further along the parched trail that ran parallel to a paved highway a half-mile to the south. *Dang, I got to get to where we need to be awful soon,* he reminded himself. *It's real important. Yup, it sure is.*

When he reached Ellsworth, he slowed to a trot and gave the Farley granary a long look. *No . . . no, can't stop to say hello. Gotta keep going,* he thought, urging his mount onward with a soft poke of his boot heels.

"C'mon ol' boy, ain't there yet. We got business to tend. So, giddup, now . . . ya' hear?"

A dozen miles later, he found himself in Lakeside.

"Place looks as worn out as I remember. 'Course, where we're headed ain't much prettier. Antioch is our stop, Rickets, and it's the next town up. Promise you that. So don't go losin' your legs yet."

By the time Billy-John reached the outskirts of his destination, his aging nag was lathered up and snorting hard. He dismounted the swaybacked Appaloosa and gave it a drink from his canteen. He then poured the remaining drops

201

of tepid water down his dry gullet as he gazed at the western horizon.

"There's the place we need to get to. Yup, that's where we're gonna', ah . . . " he mumbled, and then a look of bewilderment covered his weathered face.

After a few moments, he climbed from his horse and threw his hat to the ground.

"Shiii-*it!* If I ain't gone forgot why it is we come here."

#

Why Earthlings Confuse Extraterrestrials

It was reported that sentient beings on Earth attempted to rescue a beached 2,000-pound sea creature known for attacking and devouring them. The story stated that some human onlookers wept when the 14-foot shark died.

#

The Smell of Distress

The nose is the most powerful of the human senses. It has the ability to reclaim memories and images long tucked away. Even people in comas detect smells, or at least that's what Fergie Myerson had read, and she believed it. It was this certainty that led her to seek a method to change the way people on their deathbeds spent their final moments. She asserted that scents pleasing to those about to perish would make their passing a less traumatic, even enjoyable, experience.

After extensively researching which aromas evoked the most agreeable visceral responses in humans, Fergie offered her idea to hospice patients in the last moments of their lives. To the amazement of relatives, happiness covered the faces of their loved ones as they breathed in the mellifluent vapors of Ambrosia upon passing away. Even those who had been the most morose of patients exhibited blissfulness as they they inhaled for the last time.

Soon, Fergie's services were in such great demand that she found it necessary to hire others to take on the additional requests. This turned out to be a fateful decision on her part since one of her new staffers suffered from Anosmia and inadvertently mixed a few drops of hydrogen sulphide into the formula intended for a client. Rather than provide the dying person a bucolic departure, it so offended her olfactory senses that she punched out the priest giving her the Last Rights.

\#

Exceptional Service

A Fed Ex truck pulled out in front of me and moved very slowly down Route 6. I looked to see what was ahead of it and saw another Fed Ex truck. Then to my surprise, I noticed an endless row of Fed Ex trucks beyond it. I checked my rear view mirror, and there was a Fed Ex truck closing in on my bumper, and another trailing it. As I approached a busy intersection, a stream of Fed Ex trucks appeared from both the left and right lanes. Adding to my growing puzzlement, a fleet of Fed Ex trucks spilled onto the road from every side street I passed. Suddenly a Fed Ex truck came up along side of me—nearly colliding with an oncoming Fed Ex truck. The driver in it signaled for me to pull over. With mounting anxiety, I turned into the parking lot of a strip mall. As I climbed from my car, the Fed Ex driver did the same from his truck. In an instant, his vehicle was joined by dozens of other Fed Ex trucks, their drivers emerging from them. A look of great purpose covered their weathered faces. Before I could ask what was going on, a chorus of voices chimed: *We have a same day delivery for you, sir!*

#

Compromise

We win justice quickest by rendering justice to the other party.

—Mahatma Gandhi

Howard could stand or lie down, but he was barred from sitting.

"It's impossible to live this way," he complained to his wife, Vera.

"You knew that when we replaced the chairs in our house with brand new ones that you wouldn't be allowed to sit on them because of your barbed tail," she replied.

Howard had thought his wife's unreasonable demand would be short lived once she saw the problem it created for him. He was wrong though. It had been three weeks, and she was holding fast to her edict barring his protuberance from ever making contact with their replacement seating.

"That's all well and good for you. You don't have a prehensile spike. Can't you see I'm miserable?"

"Too bad. That thing has destroyed more furniture than I can count. I've pleaded with you for years to have it removed, but *no* you wouldn't even consider it. Your precious, precious butt spear," barked Vera.

"It's an integral part of me. Removing it would change who I am. And you know there could be complications from surgery. Besides, have I asked you to cut off your third foot?"

"It doesn't ruin the seats . . . *does* it?"

"C'mon, Vera. It's affecting the quality of my home life. I'm so tired of standing while watching television or eating or reading the newspaper. None of these things work lying down either. You know that. Please, let me . . ."

"Forget about it. You're not going to sit on our brand new chairs . . . *never!*"

It was with that emphatic statement that Howard decided to take action. *It's either her or me,* he thought, while moving to where his wife sat in her shiny red leather recliner.

"What are you doing, Howard?" asked Vera, as her husband turned his back and suddenly descended on her ass first.

The thickness of her lap kept Howard's lance-like tail from cutting into the cushion of the chair under her.

"There . . . we both got what we wanted," said Howard, as he nestled into the folds of his wife's skirt.

He took her reticence to mean that he could now sit anywhere he damn well pleased.

#

The Too Late Show

Cyril Kazan had been bothered for quite some time—at least since he'd turned 60 a half dozen years earlier—that he couldn't stay awake long enough to watch the television late night talk shows. This was also true for his wife, Kayla.

Typically the Kazans would nod off by 9:30-10 o'clock as they sat in front of their 15 year-old, 28-inch Panasonic television. This issue so gnawed at Cyril that he finally wrote the programming departments of the major broadcast networks with a suggestion that he hoped they might embrace.

His letter read as follows:

Dear Program Executive:

My wife and I are now in our 60s and find it very difficult to stay awake long enough to enjoy your late night talk show. We greatly miss and long for the glory days of Johnny Carson when we were younger—we can't tell you how much we loved Ed and Doc. For a time we watched Jay Leno, but then we began to experience drowsiness because of the late hour of the broadcast.

Would it be possible for you to schedule an "early" late night talk show designed for seniors, say beginning at 8 PM? I believe there's a huge potential audience for such an program given the aging Baby-Boomer population. This "early" late night talk show, as I'm calling it for lack of a better name, could feature hosts and guests in the same age demographic as its viewers, making it all the more relevant and appealing.

If you would give this proposal appropriate consideration, we would very much appreciate it.

Sincerely,

Cyril Kazan

Two months later, Cyril received a reply to his letter from one of the networks.

Dear Mr. Zakan,

Thank you for your programming suggestion. While we understand your frustration stemming from an inability to stay up long enough to watch our late night talk show (we realize it is difficult to be old), we're afraid we cannot comply with your request.

The reason for this is purely economic. Elderly viewers—those in their twilight years—do not appeal to sponsors, with the exception of pharmaceutical and adult diaper manufacturers. While there is profit to be made from them, it pales by comparison to that spent by advertisers wishing to reach the 24-39 year old viewer.

May we suggest a possible solution to your dilemma? You might DVR our late night talk show for viewing at an hour when you are fully conscious. If you're not familiar with this technology (and that would be understandable given your considerable age), we're sure your cable provider can explain it to you.

Very sincerely,

Donald J. Caufield, Jr.
Vice President, Audience Relations

Cyril was infuriated by what he saw was Caufield's unnecessarily demeaning response, and he dashed off yet another letter—this time sending it via Express Mail:

Dear Mr. Caulfeld, Junior,

Your message was an insult to my intelligence, and it's clear that you have an enormous gap in yours to think that only older people with medical and bladder issues can inspire advertising revenues. Furthermore, to be of the opinion that folks of a certain age are beyond grasping the rudiments of modern video technology shows just how uniformed you are about my generation.

Are you aware that the founders of your medium, David Sarnoff and William Paley, were still at the helm of their networks (NBC and CBS respectively, in case you don't know) long past their 70th birthdays? Of course, I suppose you would have held them in equal contempt because of their "mature" age.

Anyway, I don't want to take up anymore of your valuable time, as I suspect there are tremendous pressures on you to come up with more brilliant programs, like "Here Comes Honey Boo Boo" and "Toddlers in Tiaras." These network shows reflect the sad reality of your insufficient programming talent.

Finally, I've concluded that the reason why we snooze in front of the television so early is that there isn't anything stimulating enough to keep us up until your late talk show comes on.

With all due dis-respect,

Cyril K-A-Z-A-N, Senior (and proud of it)

Cyril was surprised when a week later he received an envelope from Caufield containing two complimentary tickets to his network's 1:30 AM "Late, *Late* Show."

A note accompanying the tickets read: "Hope you're *up* for this."

#

The 300th

[S]he was between stories, and [s]he felt despicable.
                              —Raymond Carver

Caitlin Holder was unable to come up with a fresh idea for what would be her 300th piece of short fiction, so she scanned her story idea file in the hope of finding something that she could expand into a new tale. The following are plot sketches from which she could choose:

~~~

Title: "A Nuclear Family" — Scenario: Family concerned about potential contamination from nearby nuclear power plant moves to remote location only to discover it has bought property only a few miles from a toxic waste dump . . .

Title: "B&W" — Scenario: Louis Cormier finds escape in his dreams wherein all humans are of one color and racial hatred does not exist. When a Jewish family moves in next-door, he puts his house up for sale . . .

Title: "Black Hole" — Scenario: Scientist Carson Perrault stumbles onto a chemical formula that changes hard objects in soft ones. When he drops some into his lap, his life is suddenly changed . . .

Title: "Blue Bungalow" — Scenario: Jason Krebs beloved wife passes away and he is left to mourn in the tiny house they had lived in for 30 years. One day he comes across a love letter she had written to someone he didn't know. He sets out to find this person . . .

Title: "Carrion Baggage" — Scenario: After seven tries, Eric Potter lands the elusive Almaco Jack off the coast of Jamaica. He carries the prized catch in a small ice chest on board his return flight. The plane is delayed several hours and the ice melts causing the fish to give off a strong odor. Passengers begin to react . . .

Title: "Coastal Flooding" — Scenario: Accelerated global warming causes oceans to rise and flow inland, creating beaches in eastern Ohio and western Nevada . . .

Title: "Do Not Look Down On Me Dead" — Scenario: A terminally ill man engages in a conversation with his wife about how he wants to be displayed at his wake. His unusual request shocks and upsets her . . .

Title: "Double Trouble" — Scenario: Felix Dopperman has a non-existing libido so purchases a robot to service his sexually voracious wife. She falls in love with the substitute lover . . .

Title: "Fun at Farley's" — Scenario: A convalescent home director realizes his clients are dying off and not being replaced. Concludes he needs to keep them alive to remain in business, so he implements an exercise program that has disastrous results . . .

Title: "His Last Happy Day" — Scenario: Man recounts the blissful 24 hours leading up to his fatal diagnosis. Decides to relive it everyday until he dies . . .

Title: "Inside Twilight" — Scenario: Earth's rotation slows causing a change in the length of daylight around the world. Population shifts as people escape longer nights in favor of longer days . . .

Title: "It's Not Unusual" — Scenario: The pain in his dorsal limb reminds Cepic Duq that it will soon detach from his body requiring his return to the renewal incubator. Before this occurs, he must consummate his marriage vows . . .

Title: "Jihadma" — Scenario: Upset by Muslim extremists' acts, Benton Manley builds explosives containing red, white, and blue confetti that he plans to detonate at Islamic mosques . . .

Title: "Landing on the Sun" — Scenario: Of all the get-rich-quick schemes Paul Gasman has come up with, his friends think his latest is the most ridiculous by far . . .

Title: "Dead Reckoning" — Scenario: A long missing burial site containing the body of a prominent historical figure is found. The town sees the discovery as a way of profiting from tourism, but the deceased person's descendants wish to relocate his remains . . .

Title: "Man's Best Friend" — Scenario: A lonely man's Golden Retriever begins to show aging as white whiskers appear on its snout. This disturbs him to the extent that he dyes the dog's facial fur. Unsettling consequences result . . .

Title: "Money to Die For" — Scenario: The state lotto is about to go bust due to bad management resulting in too many winners. It decides to knock off its yearly payoff prizewinners in order to remain afloat . . .

Title: "Nowhere Woman" — Scenario: Gale Caulkin's massive insecurities cause her to do foolish, if not outlandish, things . . .

Title: "Painless" — Scenario: Man has affliction that keeps him from feeling pain, so he decides to exploit his condition for profit. Bizarre results cause mayhem for him and his family . . .

Title: "Thump, Thump" — Scenario: As a young boy, Quinn Silva discovers that when he listens to people's heartbeats with his toy stethoscope he can see their future . . .

Title: "Flesh" — Scenario: Man that has fixation on a swimsuit model is devastated when he notices she has a tattoo covering the upper part of her left thigh. He kidnaps her in order to remove it only to discover the ink was temporary . . .

Title: "Slidin' Into Dyin'" — Scenario: Longtime country music singer Scarlet Hart has her first hit song just as she is told she has a disease that will end her life . . .

Title: "Special Delivery" — Scenario: Father of a child killed by drunk driver decides on method of revenge when court frees man. Places venomous snake in culprit's mailbox, but things don't go as distraught parent planned . . .

Title: "Wheel of Misfortune" — Scenario: After 30 years on a successful television game show, the host can no longer cope with the numbing routine of his job. Decides to sabotage program to relieve his boredom . . .

Title: "Tsunami Mommy" — Scenario: In response to Tiger Mom's Draconian approach to child rearing, a mother writes book that posits the view that chaos and lack of discipline is best way to raise children . . .

Title: "The Angry Dead" — Scenario: The deceased come back to put a better spin on the bad image that films and books have given them. They hire a PR person, who turns out to be wildly incompetent . . .

Title: "Taking the Leap" — Scenario: Chuck Fisher concludes that there isn't a really good or fitting way to leave this world when people decide to do themselves in. He decides to build a luxurious hotel atop a high cliff on a remote South Pacific island to give those interested in ending life a better alternative to the conventional methods of suicide . . .

Title: "The Insinuator" — Scenario: Thirteen year-old Davy White discovers he can enter peoples' dreams and change their outcomes. When he finds that his would-be girlfriend dreams of another boy, he uses his exceptional ability to his advantage . . .

Title: "The Pass Through" — Scenario: Discovery of a habitable sister planet by NASA astronomers launches a future probe. Astronauts that travel to what is called Tess 1 find that all of Earth's dead have been reanimated on the planet . . .

Title: "The Simoniac" — Scenario: Buying and selling sacred and spiritual objects gets Clare Marie into hot water. She buys a small figurine said to be from an extinct culture only to find it is anything but extinct . . .

"Damn, there's nothing much worth writing about here," sighed Caitlin.

And then a new idea struck her . . .

#

Can You Answer This?

Why don't publishers respond to their authors?
They have all the power, and we have only hope.
So, yes, why *don't* publishers respond to their authors?
Is it too much of a favor to ask of them?

#

Number's Up

*Never make predictions, especially about
the future.*
　　　　　　　　—Casey Stengel

Much to his amazement as well as bafflement Will Carpenter
found that he could make a certain type of dire prediction.
The 82 year-old member of the Hornsby, Idaho, senior center
appeared to possess the dubious ability to forecast when a
person would die. While he could not provide any specifics
surrounding a person's demise, Will could cite the actual day
of death. Indeed, he'd done so on three occasions just over
the past year.

When numbers first appeared over a friend's head, Will
thought that perhaps he was having one of his silent
migraines. In the past he'd seen flashing lights that distorted
objects before him. But this was different—he'd never seen
numbers just dangling in mid-air. When a second elderly
friend—who'd also had figures floating above him—died,
Will connected the dots and realized the digits formed the
date that an individual would pass.

With some reluctance, Will told his best friend, Guy La
Pierre, about his disturbing visions, hoping he'd keep them to
himself.

"That's pretty crazy, Willy. You have your eyes checked?
Didn't you say you had some problems seeing things a while
back."

"Yeah, I did. The doc told me I have these migraines that
mess up my sight, but this is different. No flashing lights . . .
just clear numbers hanging over people's heads. I figured out
what they are, too. They're dates . . . the day, month, and year
when the person standing or sitting under them is going to

die. It's happened a few times now, Guy. Saw them before Karen died and again a week before Craig had his heart attack."

"Now, that's got to be a figment of your imagination, Willy, You should get them old peepers checked out again. You never know what could be causing those, ah . . . hallucinations. Could be serious."

"They're not *hallucinations,* Guy. I see what I see and then something actually happens. I'm worried because just yesterday I saw numbers over Alex's head."

"Alex Boswell? What was the date?"

"The numbers were 9/17/15."

"Well, that's just a week or so away. Let's see if what you're saying holds up. Not long to wait."

"Should we tell poor Alex?"

"What? Tell him you've seen the date that he's going to croak dangling over his head. Shoot, Willy, he's 91! You tell him that and he'll surely die."

Will agonized over a possible course of action but in the end decided that Guy was right; there was little he could do. What was going to happen was simply going to happen . . . Then, sure enough, on the 17th of September, Alex's daughter found her father dead in his recliner.

Since Guy was bad at keeping secrets, it wasn't long before rumors spread about Will's disconcerting talent. After having correctly predicted Alex's demise, most residents of Hornsby steered clear of him, fearing he might reveal their final day. To his surprise and chagrin, the owner of the town's dry goods store, Mary Harding—a longtime friend—asked if he might determine her expiration date. At first he baulked at the very idea but then agreed to come see her because of her unrelenting insistence.

When Will entered Mary's store the next day, young Simon Burwell was there. For some reason he would never understand, Will found himself blurting out the set of numbers he saw suspended near where the man stood.

"10/21/2015!"

"What was that?" inquired Simon, taken aback.

And Will immediately realized he'd made a terrible mistake.

"Nothing . . . *nothing at all*. I was just . . . "

"Did you predict when I would die, like they say you can?" asked Simon, now with a smug grin on his face.

No . . . not really. I mean . . ."

"Well, that's just a bunch of crap anyway. Easy to predict when them old folks are gonna' cork off. Hell, anyone look at them could tell they were about to kick the bucket. You just got lucky . . . or you put some poison in their mush."

"My mind was just drifting, sorry," said Will, nervously.

"Don't let it drift too far. Might find yourself running over one of them wrinkled up ladies you fancy at that old fart center," said Simon, giving Will a sideways glance as he left the store.

"Now, what was all that about, Will? Did you see his death numbers?" asked Mary.

"Well, yes . . . I mean I may have. Not sure, really," replied Will. "So why in the heck do you want to know when you're done with it all, Mary?"

"Haven't been feeling all that chipper lately and figured I might as well know for sure so I can get this place in order. Don't want my kids to have to clean it up after me."

Will looked above her head and took a couple steps back. "Think you're out of luck, Mary. I don't see a thing."

"C'mon, Will. Look again. You saw them other folks' dates."

"Yeah, but, sorry, just don't see any numbers for you. Could be you're going to live forever, so you don't have to tidy up."

"Maybe the numbers you saw near Simon were mine. Could have been meant for me instead of him."

"No, I don't think so. If they were for anybody, they probably were meant for him. Sorry, Mary."

"Well, could you come back in a few days? Maybe the date will pop up then."

"Sure, Mary, I can do that."

Will left the store and headed home. The thought that the numbers he saw at Mary's store might have been Simon's troubled him.

And they had begun to trouble Simon as well. At first he paid little attention to his encounter with Will, but after a while he began to wonder if there was anything to what he'd heard about the old man being able to predict when someone would die. As his initial concern grew, he began to fixate on the idea that 10/21/15 was to be his final day on Earth.

That's only 3 weeks from now. Could be dead then. Jesus, what if . . .? thought Simon, gulping at a beer as he sat on the steps of his trailer. *Maybe I can do something with the time I have left. Right some wrongs.*

Over the next couple of weeks, Simon reviewed the sad path of his life and became a changed man. He gave his ex-wife the back alimony and child support he owed her, paid his long overdue bar bill, and cleaned up the rubbish that had accrued around his ancient Winnebago.

When 10/21/15 arrived he drank himself into a stupor and blacked out. When he came to, it was early the next day.

"Lordy me, I'm still alive!" he bellowed joyfully. But then he realized he was penniless as the result of all his recent good deeds. "Shit!!!!" he growled, and then heaved up on his blanket.

Meanwhile, a customer of Mary's dry goods store was surprised to find it still closed a good hour after it normally opened. She called Mary's son, Calvin, to see what had happened. Just twenty minutes later Calvin found his mother lying on the floor behind her store's cash register with no pulse.

That morning Will felt that what little energy his old body still possessed had seemed to drain away. He had all he could do to lift himself from his bed. Sitting on its edge, he caught his image in the bedroom mirror. And there above his reflection appeared the numbers 10/22/15.

"Okay," he mumbled. "Okay . . ."

He lay back on his bed, closed his eyes, and waited.

#

The Trickle Down Effect

It's raining. *Whoa* . . . it's raining hard. No, it's *really, really* coming down. It's like a hurricane. No, more like a tsunami. Zillions of drops are hitting against the skylight. Sounds like a trillion snare drums. Crap, maybe the glass will break. If it does it'll be like a waterfall coming into the house. This could be terrible . . . disastrous. Everything could get ruined. Man, I better move all the stuff that's under the skylight, and I better do it fast. Jeez, the place feels like a quadrillion pebbles are battering it. Oh no, there's a huge water spot forming at the base of the skylight! This is the start of something really bad. The whole ceiling could come down. Should get a tarp from the garage and cover everything. Holy moley, hear that? *Hear* that? It's coming down even harder now. Floods . . . there will be flooding. The whole town will be under water. Lives may be lost. Life will change as we know it for weeks until the water recedes and power is restored. Oh, shit . . . the *power.* Son of a . . . no *CSI* tonight!

#

Acceptance

We live in a rainbow of chaos.
           —Paul Cezanne

My girlfriend and me rented a tiny bungalow next to an old ten-story tenement at the end of the boardwalk in Atlantic City. The outside of our house was in need of a coat of paint and the shutters were hanging at different angles than they should, but the interior wasn't bad. The floors were a bit uneven and there was a slight leak in the bathroom ceiling. But on the plus side, there was a small wood fireplace in the kitchen and a built-in bookshelf in the front room where we put our collection of seashells and used paperbacks. Unfortunately, the bedroom window looked out onto the wall of the cement high-rise. I calculated it was about eight inches away.

We spent what was left of the first day at our new place sitting on the sagging front porch that overlooked the ocean and then turned in. Not long after, things started crashing down on the roof. The initial loud thud shocked us out of our sleep. It was followed at measured intervals by several more jarring booms that caused us to run outside to see what was happening. As we stood on the sidewalk and looked up, another object was hurled from a window of the building that towered over ours.

"Shoes!" shouted my girlfriend. "They're dropping fucking shoes on our roof."

As soon as the words slipped from her mouth, another pair descended onto the top of our squat digs.

Stunned and perturbed, I called the police and reported what was happening.

"Shoes?" asked the officer.

"Yes, shoes," I answered.

"What type?" he inquired.

"Does it matter?" I replied.

"Maybe not . . . hold on," he said.

After a few moments, he spoke again. "Well, I checked, and there's no law against that."

"What do you mean?" I asked.

"Dropping footwear from a tall building onto a smaller one is no offence, regardless of the type of shoes," he offered.

We returned to the front porch and mulled over the officer's response to our complaint. Then we re-entered our new rental and slipped under the covers of our double bed. It only took a while before we got used to the crashing sounds and went back to sleep.

#

Pro-dactive

Sam loved the book he was reading so much that he dreaded it coming to an end. To prevent what he anticipated would be days of depression after finishing it, he ran a black magic marker over the sentences of the last page while doing his best to divert his eyes.

#

ABOUT THE AUTHOR

Michael C. Keith is the author/coauthor of 30 book volumes and dozens of articles on the subject of radio and broadcast studies. His academic titles include *Radio Cultures: The Sound Medium in American Life*, *Sounds of Change: FM Broadcasting in America (with Christopher Sterling)*, *Sounds in the Dark: All Night Radio in American Life*, *Voices in the Purple Haze: Underground Radio in the Sixties*, *Waves of Rancor: Tuning in the Radical Right (with Robert Hilliard)*, *The Broadcast Century and Beyond (With Robert Hilliard)*, *Radio Programming: Consultancy and Formatics*, and *Talking Radio: An Oral History of American Radio in the Television Age*, among others. His textbook, *Keith's Radio Station* (formerly *The Radio Station*), is the most widely adopted title on its subject globally.

In addition to his non-fiction books, Keith has published over a dozen creative works, including an acclaimed memoir, *The Next Better Place*, a young adult novel, *Life is Falling Sideways*, and 11 short story collections—most recently *Bits, Specks, Crumbs, Flecks*. His fiction has been nominated for several awards, among them the Pen/O. Henry Award, Pushcart Prize, National Indie Excellence Award, and International Book Award.

He is the recipient of several accolades in his academic field, including the International Radio and Television Society's Frank Stanton Fellow Award, Broadcast Education Association's Lifetime Achievement in Scholarship Award, and the University of Rhode Island's Achievement in the Humanities Award. Keith was the first chair of BEA's Radio Division and is a professor in the Communication Department at Boston College. He is the former chair of education at the Museum of Broadcast Communication and serves on the executive advisory boards of the University of Rhode Island's Harrington School of Communication and Media and the Newton Writing and Publishing Center.

CPSIA information can be obtained
at www.ICGtesting.com
Printed in the USA
BVOW08s2152300317

479920BV00001B/5/P